W9-AYE-809

Praise for
NORMA FOX MAZER'S
When She Was Good

"A delicately wrought piece of fiction. *When She Was Good* often sounds like nonfiction. . . . Not too good to be true, but too bad to be false. It is written with a stinging clarity and conviction."
—*The New York Times Book Review*

★ "A heart-wrenching novel. The author poetically evokes a poignant, honest image of rebirth and self-reliance. Readers who wince at the heroine's abuse and rejection will find solace in her slow-but-steady emergence into a kinder world."
—*Publishers Weekly*, starred review

★ "This isn't the first time Mazer has dealt with relationships between sisters, but this book is more intricately structured and far more brutal. Its language is at once fierce and unpretentious, and it has greater emotional depth than most YA novels."
—*Booklist*, starred review

ALA Best Book for Young Adults

SLJ Best Book

ALA *Booklist* Editors' Choice

For the Best in Literature

Fallen Angels
Walter Dean Myers

From the Notebooks of Melanin Sun
Jacqueline Woodson

Make Lemonade
Virginia Euwer Wolff

My Brother Sam Is Dead
James Lincoln Collier and Christopher Collier

Plain City
Virginia Hamilton

Toning the Sweep
Angela Johnson

When She Hollers
Cynthia Voigt

When She Was Good
Norma Fox Mazer

WHEN
SHE WAS
GOOD

WHEN SHE WAS GOOD

Norma Fox Mazer

POINT

SCHOLASTIC INC.

New York Toronto London Auckland Sydney
Mexico City New Delhi Hong Kong Buenos Aires

Arthur A. Levine Books hardcover edition designed by Elizabeth B. Parisi, published by Arthur A. Levine Books, an imprint of Scholastic Press, October 1997.

ISBN 0-590-31990-6

Library of Congress number 96-35532

12 11 10 9 8 7 6 5   2 3 4 5/0

Printed in the U.S.A   01

First Scholastic Trade paperback printing, January 2000

PART I

Earthly Comfort

3

PART II

In the Reign of Pamela

63

PART III

The Doubled Moon

133

"*We are adaptable creatures.
It's the source of our earthly comfort and ...
of our silent rage.*"

— Michael Cunningham: *A Home at the End of the World*

PART I

Earthly Comfort

I didn't believe Pamela would ever die. She was too big, too mad, too furious for anything so shabby and easy as death. And for a few moments as she lay on the floor that day, I thought it was one of her jokes. The playing-dead joke. I thought that at any moment she would spring up, seize me by the hair, and drag me around the room. It wouldn't be the first time, but this time it would be deserved, my own fault, the way she always said it was. Punishment for standing there, for watching her, for letting it happen. For saying out loud, "Well, Pamela, are you going to do it? Are you going to die?"

As a little girl, I would often chant and sing two words, which I had decided were magic words. These words were *happy home,* and how I came by them I don't know, but I believed if I said and sang them often enough, it would change things — take away Mother's sadness and make Pamela nice and even turn Father cheerful. And then I would be happy.

Eventually it became clear to me that this would not happen; yet, in some part of myself, I went on believing, not in chanting words, but in magical possibilities — I think that's the way to put it. How else explain my belief that what I wanted might be out of sight now, but was possibly only a grasp beyond whatever moment I was in? How else explain how I revived that belief time after time? How else understand that I sensed this phantom thing, happiness, as something real — like a fabulous painting or statue that existed in the world, hidden from me now, but only waiting for me to come upon it? I believed this could happen any time. In an instant, the change could occur, the gift be mine. So, despite everything, I went on waiting to be happy.

I think, now, that Mother was also waiting. Day after day she lived her life and never complained, but

I saw her sometimes staring out the window. I saw her sometimes crying.

It's four years since Mother died, and it still matters to me how she feels about things. I don't want her to be unhappy with me — if the dead can be happy or unhappy. I don't know about that, but I've always felt that she's somewhere nearby. In the case of Mother, I believe in the soul's life.

Would Mother forgive me? I would like to hear her speak once more, to hear her say it. What bothers me is that I can't remember the sound of her voice. I remember other things: how the bones poked through the skin of her hands; how she held her elbows as if weighing them, held them like some good little thing she would keep to herself. Even in the heat of summer, she'd be like that, arms crossed, as if hugging herself. And I remember her saying, "Be a good girl, Em."

Every morning she said that. Standing in the doorway of the trailer, hugging her elbows, watching Pamela and me as we left to walk to the Corners for the school bus. Her words following us down the road. "Em, be a good girl. Pamela, you, too. You hear me girls?"

And every morning, Pamela: "Shut up, Ma."

And Mother, leaning out the door: "Take care of each other."

And Pamela: "Shut your stupid face, Ma."

And my feet scuffing the sand, and Mother's voice, "Em, take care of your sister, take care of Pamela."

And Pamela: "Ma, that's stupid. I'm the older one, I take care of her."

And Mother: "You hear me, Em? Be a good girl, Em."

2

Mr. Penniman has eyes like the eyes of certain dogs, either very nice dogs or scary dogs, I can't decide which. *Stupid bitch,* Pamela says in my head. *Thinking about dogs in this place!* "Well, dear, have you made up your mind?" Mr. Penniman says. He leads the way among the coffins in the crowded room. Each one has its own bench and glitters at me like a huge jeweled chest.

"Now how about this one, dear? Copper handles."

"How much?" I say.

"I don't want you to worry about money."

I nod. I know what he is doing, of course: he is selling me something like any salesman. It's disgusting, but still I like the way he is looking at me, and I can't help wondering if he thinks I'm pretty. I'm probably just as disgusting as he is.

"This model here, Miss Thurkill, is my personal favorite. We call it the Skylark."

He stands close to me. He has a basket of dark skin under each eye, and smelly breath, but his deep voice is lovely. I hope my breath is fresh. I can smell my underarm sweat. I like that smell. *Fool,* Pamela rages in my ear. *Frucking idiot. First dogs, now smells? You'll never change.*

"Lovely deep blue satin lining, dear," Mr. Penniman says. "A very popular item. One of my satisfied customers told me, 'That lining is the color of the sky on a sunny day, Mr. Penniman.'"

I think about leaning against his chest. He could pet my head, make the choice for me. I could go to sleep right there, standing up. I love to sleep. The year Mother died, I loved it so much I slept all the time.

"And she said, 'I know my husband is happy I'm choosing something beautiful for his final resting place.' Did your sister enjoy nature, Miss Thurkill?"

"Sometimes she watched nature shows on TV."

"Get the best, dear." His hands touch the wood, caress it. "No veneers. One hundred percent natural. You won't regret it," he says. "My advice to the bereaved is to think long-term."

The BEREAVED, Pamela says. *What kind of idiot word is that?* Now she's not so mad. I can hear her laughing. She liked the big goofy words people used so they didn't have to say the little hard words. My hand goes to my breast. The bruise where the frying pan hit me is still tender.

"Miss Thurkill, special touches like the color of the lining are, psychologically speaking, important. I've been in this business a long time and, frankly, I know that doing things the right way sets the heart at ease."

He looks at me with his dog's eyes. Friendly eyes. That's it — I'm sure of it — his eyes are friendly.

"Life is long," he says. His voice rumbles through his chest. "The moment is short. Everyone's time comes. There is a season. A time to live, a time to die."

"I heard that on the radio," I say. "They were singing it. It could be the special song of funeral directors."

He doesn't give me even a tiny smile in return. He looks down, as if I did something crude: farted the way Pamela did, anywhere, anytime. It's natural, she'd say, what the hell is wrong with that? You telling me you don't fart?

Mr. Penniman smooths down his tie, which has red, white, and blue stripes. If I say it's a patriotic tie, he won't smile at that, either. Of course it's not very funny, just a tiny remark. I could tell him one of Pamela's jokes. *What's yellow and smells like carrots? Bunny farts.* It's a stupid joke: she liked anything about farts. Even if it wasn't a stupid joke, he wouldn't laugh. It's his job to be serious.

It was the same with me and Pamela. Not that living with her was a job, but of course I couldn't just laugh anytime I felt like it. I had to be mindful of the expressions on my face and the thoughts in my head. Thoughts were always a problem. There were too many times she walked into my head and stood there and saw what I was thinking. My solution was not to think anything, if possible.

I wonder if Mr. Penniman ever had sex in a coffin. It's not really an original thought. I saw it in a vampire movie we'd rented. Pamela was offended; she said it was dirty stuff for a family movie. She got mad and threw her dinner at the wall. I'd made spaghetti with tomato sauce. "Did you hear that, Em?" I got the cleanser and a sponge and began cleaning the wall. "Did you hear the dirty stuff they said?" she screamed.

She, herself, usually never said anything worse than

"bitch" or "damn." Other words she changed. She said "creezus jist" and "farsehole." She made up her mind to do that after we left the trailer and the country. The trailer stood alone in a bit of woods, back from the road that ran like an arrow to Lake Ontario. Only fishermen traveled the road, throwing up billows of dust as they sped toward the lake. When Pamela and I moved down to Syracuse, she said we had to mind our manners — funny coming from her — and she changed the way she said certain words. "Sheeeet," she said now, and "huck it." It sounds nicer, she told me, and just right for city living, and she didn't see why everyone couldn't speak the same way.

Once she heard a guest on the Phil Donahue show say "intercourse," and she was so irritated she butted her behind into the TV and knocked it over.

"Which one will it be, dear?" Mr. Penniman says. "Now is the time to pave the way for ease of mind and peace in your soul. Have you made your decision?"

My eyes are aching, as if they've been boiled like eggs. Why can't we just dig a big hole and put Pamela in it? A nice square hole, with the sides scraped down straight and neat. Like putting her in a bed, hands folded across her chest, legs straight, eyes closed. She would look peaceful. And I wouldn't have to make any decisions.

Mr. Penniman is stroking the coffin with the blue

satin lining. It has a blue satin pillow too. "Buying the best for Sister will soothe the grief." He strokes the silky pillow. "Shall we go for this one?"

I like that pillow. I would like to have it for my own. I could put my cheek against it at night and go to sleep and not think about anything, just feel the softness.

"Well, dear?"

I shake my head. Never in all the world could I afford that. I hope he doesn't try to make me buy it. I look out the window. There's wet fog hanging in the trees like gray rags. Pamela hated this month: she said March was filthy, even the rain was filthy. Once, in a good mood, she made up a song. "I'm marching because I hate March!" She went around the room, pumping her arms up and down, singing that over and over. I marched with her and sang too, and we laughed and laughed.

Really, though, I'm fond of March; I like it in a special way, because it's like no other month. March is March. It's like nothing except itself. It's muddy and it's foggy and it's awful, and you can never mistake it for any other month.

"Dear. We must come to a decision."

I feel a cough coming, but no decision. I press my hand flat against my throat, but the cough starts

anyway, a dry choky thing. *Just stop stop stop STOP.*
You're doing that frucking cough to make me crazy.

"I am not. I'm not," I protest.

"Excuse me?" Mr. Penniman says.

"I have to have the cheapest one," I get out.

"Ahhh." His eyes are doors closing.

He swivels away from me, walks toward his office,
and I follow. I've disappointed him. He's spent all this
time with me, and there's not going to be a good sale.
At least he didn't yell.

No one has yelled at me for two days. Ever since.
I'm no longer used to such quiet. Morning and night,
quiet, so quiet. Even the furniture is quiet. It was
quiet that way in the country when we all lived together. Mother used to say, "It's too quiet here!" We
were a mile off the paved road. There wasn't even a
sign for our road, but everyone around called it the
Killenhorn Road for the family that owned the gravel
pit. They had let Father put his trailer on the land
years ago, even before Pamela was born. Or maybe
not. Maybe he just did it, and they didn't care. We
didn't take up much space. It was just us and our
trailer on a rise over the stream.

Sometimes, in good weather, Mother would go
outside at night and walk up and down the road. I can
see her, arms crossed, kicking at the sand. I can see

myself standing by an open window, watching and listening. Sometimes she would speak to herself or cry out. Once she cried, "Help!" And another time I heard her say, "It's quiet as the grave here!"

"Are you talking to yourself?" Father would come and stand in the doorway. "What are you doing, Veronica?"

"Nothing. Walking."

"Come inside. You'll get sick."

"No, no, I'm fine."

Up and down she'd go. In the spring, the peepers clattered. I miss the peepers in the city. In the summer, it was cicadas, a sound like electric wires. In the winter, nothing but wind and fat cakes of snow everywhere. Mother never went out in winter, except to go to work. It was spring and summer when she paced the road. When she said, "It's quiet as the grave around here. What am I doing in this place, with no one except the frogs and the bugs?" When I stood by my window, watching her, thinking, *Mother, I'm here. I'm here too.*

Quiet as the grave, that's the apartment. But it's not a grave. There's no one dead in it now. Unless I am. It could be that I'm dead and don't know it. *Shut up! You are never going to make it without me, you pathetic loony.*

On TV, a few years ago, I saw pictures of an earthquake in Chile. First, the buildings — which looked solid enough to last forever — fell. They fell in every direction, spraying and crumbling. They fell like paper. Like dust. Like toys. Everything was falling. Streets caved in, swallowing the world. Bricks and sticks and cars and refrigerators and people disappeared. There was dust everywhere. A strange silence. Then the cries of people. What must they have been saying? Then the rescuers, the sound of sirens, the dazed survivors rubbing at the spot where their hearts were supposed to be.

"What will be the form of payment?" Mr. Penniman sits at his desk. He pats his tie from top to bottom. "Cash, check, or charge card?"

I open my purse. Inside is the white bank envelope. I count out the bills slowly. I don't want to give him this money, but I do, and then the envelope is thin.

"Now what have we missed?" His voice is friendly again. "Do you have someone for the service? I recommend Kevin Fletcher. Nondenominational, does a super job. You'd never guess he didn't know the deceased intimately." He makes a note on a pad. "Will the coffin be open during the service, dear?"

My head heats up in two paths of fire. Suddenly I understand that Pamela is going to be put in a box, and it will make her furious. She will rise up, she will burst out, she will curse me and take me by the throat and pull me into the box with her. My heart stabs at my ribs. I know this can't be true, but what if it is? "I want the box locked," I say.

"A lock is not available on the model you've chosen. But, Miss Thurkill!" Mr. Penniman smiles at last, thrilled with his joke. "Don't worry! No one that I know of has ever gotten out."

3

"Today the sun is shining and the leaves are pretty and shiny," I wrote in the journal I kept for eighth-grade English. I always tried to write nice things, pretty things. "Today, I found a salamander, it was red as the sunset. . . . The birch trees are like dancing girls in the wind."

I never wrote about Pamela or Mother and Father or the trailer. I knew Mrs. Karyl would not like to read about such stuff. She was tall and had a bird's nest of thick black hair. She read poetry to us and as she talked, she pushed her pencil into her nest of hair: in and out, in and out. That gesture fascinated me and I imitated it whenever I was alone, poking a pencil into my own thick black hair.

"Have you written in your journal today, class?" she said each day. "Remember to be honest. No faking it. Your inner truth, that's what a journal is for."

"My inner truth is that my stomach feels rotten," Peter Hamilton said. Everyone laughed, of course. I wondered what it must feel like to make other people laugh, to have them look at you as if you were special. No one had ever looked at me that way for anything I did.

But then, I did so little. I sat in the back of the room and didn't speak. I felt I had nothing to say. Then, one day, I wrote a handful of words in my journal that surprised and frightened me. These words seemed to scribble themselves onto the paper, to pour out of my pen without any direction from me. I wrote the first word, and the others followed as if they were on a line and I was only pulling it. "Light," I wrote, and then here came the others, "at night is sometimes green and sometimes bright and sometimes pale and white." My pencil shook across the paper. "I wonder if, like birds and words, I could fly in that white green light?"

I left my journal on Mrs. Karyl's desk at the end of the period. The next day she was waiting for me. "Em."

She put her hand on my arm. "You wrote something fine, Em." Her eyes shone at me. "That's so amazing, Em. Do more! Keep it up!"

She had never noticed me before and a thought entered my mind: I did something good. No, better than good. *Amazing*. Amazing — even though Mother had died the winter before while I slept like a pig, never knowing she was leaving me forever. Amazing — even though Father sat on the couch night after night without speaking, his long bony head held between his hands. Amazing — even though Pamela said daily how she hated my sad stupid face, and did I know that I looked like a piece of old green crap.

I started carrying the notebook with me all the time, on the school bus, at home, in the bathroom, in every class. I slept with it under my pillow, my hand on it, believing that sleep might bring me something fine. Everything I wrote in it disappointed me, but every day I wrote something, and every day I hoped for something to show Mrs. Karyl.

"What're you doing?" Pamela said one day.

"Nothing." I was in the kitchen, sitting at the table. I closed the notebook.

"Don't give me that crap. Show me what you're doing."

"It's just something for school, Pamela."

"You're lying. You're always writing in that thing."

She raised her hand and smiled at me, as if we shared a secret about that hand. And maybe we did. Since Mother died, she had taken to slapping me now and then.

"Give me that notebook," she said.

"It's nothing. It's junk," I said, my heart jerking at the betrayal of the notebook I loved. "Just some old junk."

"I don't want you writing junk. Or anything. You hear me?"

"I hear you."

"Okay."

After that I tried to write in the notebook only in school, but there were moments when I was careless, when I felt I had to write even though I was at home. So it should have been no surprise when, one night, Pamela walked into the room we shared and caught me at it. She stood in the doorway. "Didn't I tell you not to do that?"

"Pamela, it's my notebook for school."

"Give that here."

I was sitting on the floor. I noticed her hands: they were puffy, like a couple of rolls.

"Give it to me," I said.

"It's for the teacher, Pamela; it's for Mrs. Karyl."

"Mrs. Crapel, you mean."

She came toward me. She had a big, rolling sort of

walk. She was big anyway, heavy boned, her thighs large and womanly. Her walk puffed her up bigger. I held my notebook against my chest. I tried to defend it, but she took it from me easily.

She flipped through it, snorting. "I hate crap like this. All this secret writing stuff. You shouldn't have secrets from me, I'm your sister." She went out of the room with the notebook.

"What are you going to do?" I scrambled after her. "Pamela, what're you doing?"

She was in the bathroom, tearing it up, flushing the bits of paper down the toilet.

"Stop!" I grabbed at her arm. She pushed me away and went on tearing and flushing.

4

Into the shower and out — fast, fast — as if Pamela's in the other room shouting for me to hurry. Listening, listening, always listening for her. Drying myself fast, breasts tiny and soft floating across my chest. Pretty? Are they pretty? *Filthy filthy stop that get your mind out of the gutter.* I look at myself in the mirror, look closer, look at my face. After Mother died, Father's face shrank, grew smaller, flesh tightening against his skull. Strangely, he didn't look older, but like the younger brother of himself.

My left eye bulges at me. It might not be mine *are you crazy* might be Pamela's. Mother once said the dead always leave something behind them.

CALL THE FUNNY FARM, LOCK HER UP!

My stomach thumps with quick beats. Will she never stop, never be quiet? I pull on clothes, run out. Must get away, away from her, from her voice, her voice always telling me telling me telling me.

"Hello, Em!" William, on the bench in the lobby as I fly past.

"Hello, William." Open the door. Get out. Get away.

"This is my place, Em."

"I know, William."

"This is where I sit."

"Yes. I know."

His voice darts after me, trying to snag me. "You can sit here too. You're pretty. Are you happy today, Em?"

Yes, oh yes, William, I'm so happy. Why does he always ask me that? I walk around the side of the building, across the grass strip and into the field. Waste field stretching a city block. It belongs to the university. People say they'll build something here someday. Now it's nothing but weeds, stones, trash. Pamela didn't like the rough ground. She hated the stones. It made walking difficult. "Remember the sand on our road," she'd say. It was the only time I ever heard her speak about our old life with regret. "Remember how you could walk down that road barefoot in the good weather?" She never came to this field, never. It used to be my special place, but this last year, after I came back from Vermont, she wouldn't let me out of the apartment for anything, not even a walk. Every day was the same. The same walls, the same rooms, the same TV shows, the same food, same words, same blows, everything the same.

I kick aside a beer can, walk swiftly. So good to walk. So good to walk across a big space, to breathe air, to look around, to keep going, to think of nothing.

At the other end of the field, I push through a tangle of bushes and come out on Davis Avenue. Nice neat Davis Avenue. Nice houses, nice lawns, nice people, nice children, nice parents, everything nice. Not like me. Me and Pamela. We are not nice. Not normal, not regular. We are crazy, dirty, stupid, and nobody must know. Nobody nobody. *Did you talk what did you tell them keep your frucking mouth shut.* In my chest, something alive, chewing on me, like mice — softly softly chewing, noiseless, soft, steady chewing.

I don't want to go back to the apartment, not if she's there, not if her voice is there. I won't stop, just keep walking like this, walking away from her, swinging my arms, passing the pretty houses. I would like to walk like this forever, thinking of nothing, only going forward, moment by moment, hour by hour, day after day. I could walk across the country from here, the middle of New York State, to California *crazy you are crazy* down the coast — the beautiful rocks and ocean, I've seen the pictures — across to Texas *you're gone a goner over the edge* Louisiana, Florida, up the East Coast, all the states, Georgia, North Carolina, Maryland *crazier and stupider every day your brains are spaghetti* — "Stop," I cry into the air. "Shut up, Pamela, I want you to shut up," I plead.

5

"Thurkill," I say, holding the phone close to my mouth. "I want to leave a message for him. He'll come in and —"

"Who?" the man says.

"Thurkill," I say again, making it two clear syllables. "Raymond Thurkill. He's my father," I add, as if that will help the man's hearing. We had always picked up our messages at the grocery store at the crossroads that everyone called the Corners, but this man is new, and I have to repeat Father's name again and then spell it. "Thurkill. T-H-U-R-K-"

"Thursday?" he says. "I can't hear you so good. Speak up, will you?"

"Thurkill."

"Thurkis?"

"Kill. 'Kill' like 'die'!"

When I hang up, I'm trembling: I feel strange and wild. I wanted to scream at that man. I wanted to leap through the phone and get my hands around his throat. I pace up and down the room. The furniture watches. Pamela's chair leers smugly. I can still see the imprint of her in the cushion.

Will Father get the message? Is he even still alive? I've sent him postcards, but there's never been a reply. Not once in four years. I think of falling on the floor and pounding my heels until Mr. Foster downstairs bangs the ceiling with his broom handle. I think of lying there, staring at the ceiling or at nothing. Lying without moving or eating or speaking. Without breathing. But it's not possible. I have tried it, and I know that the body has a will of its own. You may want not to breathe, but the body breathes, and it forces you to breathe with it.

I reach for the phone. Mary Uth is the one other person I can think of who might want to know about

Pamela. "You have reached 693–5593," her voice says on the answering machine. "Leave a message after the beeps." Then there's a snort and a giggle. "Not bad for an old lady of seventy-five, huh?" she says. "Now watch those beeps. A lot of them."

Six, in fact. "Uh, hello," I say, "this is Em Thurkill." And think how stupid I am; think why should Mary Uth care if Pamela is dead or alive?

Mary Uth is Mother's fourth, or maybe fifth, cousin. She's seventy-five and so far as I know my only relative. We met once, not too long after Pamela and I moved into this apartment. I had found my first job and I wanted, I think, to show us off to someone. Here we were in our own apartment, with food in our refrigerator. Doing good, I thought, and I looked up Mary Uth's number in the phone book. I called several times, whenever I could without Pamela's noticing, but hung up as soon as I heard the answering machine.

One day, finally, she answered. I told her who I was. "Veronica's daughter," I said.

"Oh yes," she said. Oh yes, she would come to see us.

I was curious to meet her, and happy. She would be our first visitor. She was our cousin. I remembered Mother talking about her, and I thought that Mother would be glad if she knew. I didn't tell Pamela about the visit, though. I guess I thought to surprise her. What could have been in my mind? Did I really think I would please Pamela? She was flabbergasted when Mary Uth appeared, and then furious. She screamed a long scream, a long stream of insults and abuse. *Old bitch frucking bag of bones did you ever come to see our mother do you even care she died get that disgusting ugly face away from me or I'll puke on your head.*

Mary Uth was an old woman, an old skinny woman with a small beaky face, like a skinned baby bird. Her thin old mouth opened in surprise. She looked at me, buttoning her coat back up with hands spotted with dark age marks. Pamela, I said, Pamela don't. Don't, Pamela. She took Mary Uth by the shoulders, shoved her out the door, slammed it, and went after me. She dragged me around by my braid, thumping my head until she was worn out and crying. That was the signal it was over. Then there was ice wrapped in a washcloth and the darkness of the room, and the trembling, and finally the long hard sleep. A few days later I began to cut my hair: I did it in secret, bit by bit. She never noticed until it was too late.

That is what I think of now as, for the second time, I leave a message on Mary Uth's answering machine, telling her that Pamela has died and there is going to be a service in two days.

*   *   *

"Hard to make up your mind, isn't it?" the man says. We are looking at toothbrushes in the drugstore. We have arrived in this aisle at the same moment, but from opposite directions. I wonder if the bristles on his old toothbrush are as splayed out as mine; they're like drunk dancers *what the hell are you babbling about now* OR RAGGEDY FENCEPOSTS I shout silently at her. The light in the drugstore is white, blaring, like a horn that won't stop. What am I doing in here anyway? Why am so I intent on buying a new toothbrush today? There are two dozen other things I could have done, should be doing. A hundred other things, a thousand other things. Tomorrow is my sister's funeral, and I'm standing here trying to find the perfect, the exactly right, toothbrush.

"I always have toothbrush trouble," the man says. He has eyes like a baby. Round, brown, and staring. He's wearing a checkered sports jacket and baggy dark blue pants. "Which size, which color, which brand? So many decisions," he says, popping his eyes.

Maybe I'm buying a toothbrush because I want to bury my old one tomorrow. Two funerals. Toothbrush funeral, Pamela funeral. She was always nagging me to get more "mileage" out of my toothbrush. As if it was a car, the car she would never agree to buy. *Damn right it's my money you want to throw around.*

Not now it isn't, I say.

The man blinks at me. Did I say it out loud? I pick up a toothbrush. It says LONG HEAD on the box. Father has a long head. Is that better than a short head? What kind of head do I have? Stop, I tell myself, stop thinking like this.

"This is a good drugstore," the man says, waving a hand over the rows of colored toothbrushes like a benediction. St. Toothbrush. "Definitely pro choice," he says, giving me a sly smile.

I like his joke, but mine is better. Two funerals. He's looking at me, waiting for me to say something. My turn. That's the way you do it. First one person speaks, then the other. I could tell him about the funerals. The checks in his jacket vibrate under the glassy light, and I realize I hate checks. Checks and plaids both. Why is he talking to me? He seems okay, but how can you be sure about these things? How can you be sure of anything?

My eyes throb. I grab a toothbrush, the first one my hand finds, not even a nice color. He's saying something. I nod as if I'm listening, then walk away, past the shelves of hair oil and soap and perfume, and I'm thinking that I don't know how to act around people anymore. I feel like crying, but I don't know how to do that anymore, either.

6

The sky is powdery blue after last night's rain. The custodian's stone cottage gleams as if it's just been washed. If you didn't notice all the gravestones, you'd think you were someplace enchanted. In the middle of the city, the cemetery, with its birch and oak trees is like something out of a fairy tale. "Hansel and Gretel," maybe. I always liked that story, but I wanted them to keep going, go far enough to get away from the wicked witch, far far away.

A car comes down the road and parks. Two people

get out, a man and woman wearing matching dark blue overcoats. The woman unfurls a red umbrella and holds it up, as if to fend off torrents of rain or maybe witches. Or maybe bad luck. Is the umbrella good luck? Is red a good-luck color? Pamela hated red. Once I had to throw away a pair of socks because they had red toes. The man and woman walk slowly by me.

Another car clatters to a stop, and I raise my hand, call out. It's my cousin, Mary Uth. She gets out of the car and begins wiping the dust off the windshield with a cloth. She wipes the headlights, front and back, and then does the windshield again. "I'm particular about my car," she says.

I wanted a car, but Pamela wouldn't hear of it. What for? she said. So we can take a drive, I said. Where? she said. Anyplace, I said. It doesn't matter. Just a drive, Pamela. In the country maybe, to see things. You wouldn't have to get out or anything. No, she said. No car. I don't like cars, and I don't like going places and having to see people. Forget it.

Mary Uth folds the cloth carefully into a plastic bag, puts the plastic bag into the shiny black handbag hanging over her shoulder, and walks toward me. "Em?" She puts out a bony hand and peers into my face, as if to be sure it's me. Her eyes are small, red streaked.

"Hello, cousin Mary Uth. I didn't know you were coming."

"I got your message," she says. "Still too skinny, aren't you?"

Am I? I look down at myself, see my feet in the old black shoes. Feet look enormous.

"I have to say I was one surprised party. I didn't think anything could finish that one off. Too mean to die, like they say, no offense. Is anyone else here from the family?"

The "family"? What is that? There was a family once. Four of us. Now it's something else, some creature or thing that's been reduced, or changed, or maybe no longer exists. Am I a family, me alone?

The minister arrives then, bounding boyishly out of his car. "Hello! I'm Kevin Fletcher." He does something complicated with my hand, shakes and pats and squeezes it. A ministerial handshake. He has fine, floppy hair and a jaw that angles off to one side. "Tell me about your sister. I want to say something meaningful about her, Em." He hums my name, Emmm, and draws me to him with that hum. I think Mother might have said my name that way.

"You were special to each other, and now death has parted you," he says. "What can you tell me about your sister?"

Nothing, I think, nothing at all. What is there to say about Pamela? She is gone. That's what matters. Do we have to talk? Can't we just bury her and get this over with?

"What was she like? What do you want me to say about her, Em? Tell me any little thing. Just speak about her in a natural way, anything you can think of, so I can get a feeling for her character."

What can I tell this man that won't be disgusting, appalling? I focus on the patterns of threadlike marks in the soft mud. Maybe birds' feet left those marks. Or mice. Or moles. There must be something to say, I think, as he waits, as Mary Uth looks at me knowingly, as a familiar tide of heat and shame rises across my back, a tide that will leave behind (I know this as I know my name), a trail of red bumps that will itch tormentingly, as if a horde of minuscule horses has galloped in a frenzy across my skin, rubbing it raw with tiny muscular hooves.

"What sort of person was your sister?" Kevin Fletcher is saying. "A sociable person?"

Mary Uth makes a noise in her throat.

"Kind?" he suggests. Is he really a minister? He doesn't look that much older than me. "Friendly? Those are just suggestions, Em. Tell me anything you want."

A smile fixes itself on my face. "She was Pamela," I say. My back itches mercilessly. I look down the road, searching for the hearse from the funeral home. "My sister."

"Yes, yes," he encourages, as if I have delivered tidbits of fascinating information.

I lean against a tree and, like a dog, rub against it, appeasing the itch. "We lived together." I can't seem to control the fake smile. Pamela's smile was real, made your heart jump when it appeared. The surprise of it. The relief. The second surprise of her teeth: small, like baby teeth, and white, very white. It must have been in her genes. She never brushed, she said it was a waste of time, but her teeth were beautiful.

"She was an older sister?" he says.

"Yes."

"A sister is someone to lean on." He steeples his hands under his chin. "It will be difficult for you now. You'll need to be brave."

Mary Uth pats my arm. "Yes, she will."

My nod is as false as my smile. I'm not brave. I don't know how to be brave. I'm scared all the time. Could someone tell me how to do it? There's a secret to it, something that other people know and I don't. There are secrets to everything and no one has told them to me.

"What did she do in her spare time, Em?"

I try to answer, but get stuck on the concept of "spare time." Wasn't all Pamela's time spare time? "She liked to sit," I say at last.

His expression slips; he frowns as if I'm being sly. In fact, I'm just being accurate. They must have had to stuff her into the coffin. This last year she had become fatter than ever. Fat was on her everywhere, pillows of fat on her arms and neck and around her waist and ankles. She liked being fat. She liked having massive arms and legs. She liked eating and sitting and doing nothing. She had one chair in front of the TV and one by the window, where she could watch the parking lot. When I cleaned, I had to lift the chairs, a leg at a time, so as not to jar them from their appointed places.

Her favorite chair was the one in front of the TV, and when she left it to sit in the other chair, she had a special joke. "Em!" she'd call. "I'm taking my exercise now."

"What were her hobbies? Did she dance, sing?"

"Sing, sometimes."

"Good, good! How about the arts of, you know, uh, say, embroidery?"

"She didn't do that." I feel sorry for him. With each question, he looks freshly hopeful.

"Is there anything else you can think of?"

"She liked to watch TV. She followed all the shows."

He taps his fingers on the car, smiles weakly. "Good, good," he says again. "And what about you?"

"Me?"

"You must have some hobbies. Did your sister share your hobbies with you?"

"I have no hobbies."

"Well, then. All right, we'll say something." He pats my shoulder. "It'll be good, Em."

And it is. Good enough anyway. "Pamela was a sister among sisters," he says at some point, then he says it again. He seems to like this phrase, and throws it in at least once more. Mary Uth stands next to me and occasionally squeezes my arm. The man and woman I saw getting out of the car are here also. I wonder why. Do they just like funerals? I wonder how many funerals they attend, and how often. Once a week? Every day? The woman holds up her red umbrella steadily, as if in a downpour.

Kevin Fletcher says other things that also sound good. "Pamela and Em shared a home. . . . It was a special life they led. . . . Two sisters together." No lies here. This is skill. I find myself wishing Pamela could hear him. "A sister is missed and mourned in a special way," he says. "Gone, but never forgotten." A flock of birds streaks over our heads, uttering soft hissy calls. Everyone looks up, and Kevin Fletcher seizes the moment. "God's creatures come to say good-bye to Pamela," he cries, and he lifts his clasped hands. "Good-bye, sweet sister, good-bye."

That's a little too much, I think, but Mary Uth shakes my arm and I bow my head, and make an effort at prayer. *God, keep my sister's soul, make her not suffer in hell. Hypocrite,* Pamela hisses in my ear. For once she's right.

Kevin Fletcher nods for me to pick up the shovel. "Hold on, girl," Mary Uth says. Does she mean hold on to the shovel or hold on in general? She works in an old people's home. Maybe this is what she says to keep them from dying too fast. *Hold on.* I didn't say that to Pamela when she fell off the chair. I didn't say anything. I stood above her and watched her mouth open and close soundlessly.

The dirt I shake off the shovel rattles like rain on the coffin, and the woman with the red umbrella jerks her shoulders as if offended by the sound. Kevin Fletcher nods for me to throw in another shovelful, and I bend over, digging into the pile, wondering if Pamela's mouth is still open, the way it was that day. Opening and closing, and for the first time in her life nothing coming out. Not a word, not a curse, not a cry, not a sound. But they wouldn't leave her mouth open, I'm sure of that, I've read that they tie the jaws of the dead shut, I've seen pictures of it too: there was one of a man in a coffin, it was in Ireland I think, with a white scarf tied around his head and knotted on top. It gave him a jaunty look.

A backhoe parked nearby rumbles to life and then begins to shake and grind slowly toward us. A huge rusted yellow machine with enormous muddy tires. A man in a red shirt negotiates the levers with a satisfied look on his face.

Kevin Fletcher walks me away. "There," he says. "Do you feel closure, Em?" I remember the money I'm supposed to give him. I hand it to him and say thank you. "My pleas —" he begins, then reddens and tucks the bills into his pocket. The woman with the red umbrella passes. She hasn't once looked at me.

"Good-bye," I call suddenly to her and the man with her. "Good-bye! Good-bye, Hansel and Gretel!"

They don't look at me then, either, and no one says anything, and maybe I didn't call in quite that way after all. Maybe I only wanted to. There have been so many things I've wanted to do and not done. This is probably just one more.

7

I sit on the edge of my bed and stare at the floor. I woke as tired as when I went to sleep; it was from thinking of things all night long. All night my dreams were thought-dreams, and I woke up feeling almost nauseous from so many thoughts. They rise in my mind like fireworks, sparkling and exploding, scattering bits of light and then dark into my mind.

I make myself get up, shower, dress. Now I should eat, then go outside. I have to tell myself what to do. I've done everything I had to, got Pamela buried and sent her clothes to the Salvation Army and scrubbed and cleaned the apartment. Now what? Nearly two weeks have passed. A long time, or is it a short time? Should I be happy by now? Yesterday, on the radio, a woman said, Be kind to yourself. I should have called her up and asked, How do you do that? Do I have to go to Vermont again? That's where I was kind to myself. One week of kindness.

If only there was something I had to do. Always before, I had to think of Pamela: it kept me from thinking of other things. Always there was Pamela, and now there is no Pamela. What can it mean? It is too strange. I was born into a world of Pamela. Pamela's screams, her laughter and curses. She was the mean queen of my world. The reign of Pamela was established, unquestionable. Like any queen she was extra-large, took up more space, made rooms rattle with her clamor, and dictated to one and all. Somewhere along the line, though, she became more dog than queen, seized my life between her teeth and held on as if it were nothing but a meaty bone intended for her.

For an instant, I seem to understand everything.

But what's the point of all this? What's the point of thinking so much? You think about something and you get nowhere and nothing changes, and then you feel even worse than when you started. Take my name. Em. Me. Me without the *e*. *M. M. M.* What does it mean that my name can be whittled down to a single letter? What does it signify? What if that letter were obliterated? What does it mean, in fact, that things like this go through my mind? I don't suppose I'm crazy, although she said I was. Crazy, she said, fool, idiot, moron. She said all that, she said she protected me, she said no one else understood me and that when she hit me it was my fault, I drove her to it with my stupidity and nagging. She said so many things, and I remember them all.

I remember how she tore up my notebook. How sometimes, after that, words would come into my mind that I couldn't forget. Words like the scraps of paper she'd flushed away, tiny jagged bits of things. How I wrote them down, took them out of my mind and put them on paper. Not in a notebook, oh no, a scrap of paper only, which I would keep for a while, hiding in my pocket, then tear up and flush away myself. She never knew about this. For once I put it over on her, and I thought this was wonderful. A victory. I thought it was wonderful that I could tear up and throw away my things myself. Then, gradually, I saw that it wasn't wonderful, that it was awful. And so I stopped altogether, and I didn't see that this was even more awful. I stopped. I thought I didn't have to write anything anymore. It was useless anyway. Mother was dead; it was all a mess.

Then it happened again — words appearing — and she caught me at it. We'd left Father and Killenhorn Road by then. We were here in our apartment and I was making a shopping list, writing on the back of an envelope. We never bought paper, always used the backs of things, advertisements and junk mail. MILK, I wrote, EGGS, BOLOGNA. Then the other words came, spilling from the soft black mouth of the pencil. *Heart you are eating me like a piece of meat.* Strange words, but I recognized them, as you do someone who has been sitting quietly in the back of a room and then rises and comes toward you. These words had been in my mind for days, unmoving, waiting. What are you doing? she said. What are you writing?

I slid my arm across the paper, a mistake. She rose from her chair, like a mountain rising. It made my heart beat like crazy to see her explode out of her chair. She snatched the paper and read it. She read the words out loud. She was outraged. "What is this?" The craziness of it, the weirdness, offended her. Her big hand whipping through the air. Right cheek. Left cheek. The symmetry of it. She could never stop once she began. I was on the floor, hearing her wails of grief: Why? Why? Why did you make me do it?

And later, lying in bed, ice pressed against my face, listening to music, the music Mother liked — old music,

Art Garfunkel singing in his achingly sweet voice, "... when darkness comes and pain is all around ..." Cymbals, piano. And for a moment, believing it, believing that someone might lay himself down for me like a bridge over troubled water.

It wasn't always that way. There were the other times, too, the not-so-bad times, and the good times, and even the really good times. There were the mornings when I woke and saw the silvery early light sliding under the shade and couldn't resist its pull. Come out, the light said. Come out! And I would push the covers aside, quietly, so quietly, like a mouse, with barely a rustle. One foot touching the floor, waiting, watching her in the other bed, then the second foot sliding down. Quiet, quiet. Sometimes I made it. I got out of the apartment and walked up the hill to the cemetery to watch the sunrise.

But mostly, even in her sleep, she was watching me, and as I stood up, her eyes would open. "What're you doing?"

"Nothing. I thought I'd just go out for a bit. For a walk. To see the sun rise."

"What's so fascinating about the sun? It does the same damn thing every day. It comes up and it goes down."

"It's not just the sun, Pamela. It's the morning, it's the light."

45

"The liiight." She mimicked my voice. "What about the liiight? What do you do out there in your precious liiight?"

How could I say that I didn't do anything when I went out? Looked at the sky. Smelled the air. How could I say that in the morning, my heart beat differently? That there was nothing to say, no way to put into words how it felt to walk into the coolness of the morning alone.

One morning, though, she got up and put on her shoes and said since I was always talking about the sunrise, she would see it for her own self. "See what the big damn fuss is all about." It was cold that morning, she wound scarves around her face, wore two hats and mittens. She panted as we climbed the hill toward the cemetery.

I pointed to show her where the sun was going to come up, and as I stretched out my arm, the red rim slid up from the earth.

"Hey!" Pamela said. "Hey!" I held my hand steady, finger pointing, claiming the magic, and the sun obediently slid up and up and up. "Hey," she breathed again, and tucked her arm around my waist. We stood that way, until the sun was fully up, and then we turned and went back.

8

At the Corners, when I get off the bus, I'm thirsty. I buy a soda in the store, drink it there, and then start walking. I stay to the side of the road and don't look at the cars passing. Sometimes a head turns clear around to stare at me. Am I being recognized? *Oh, that's the Thurkill girl, the younger one, the one who ran away with her crazy sister.* We never came back after we left. It's been a long time, four years, and I'm different now, aren't I?

But when I turn onto Killenhorn Road, I see that

even if I have changed, nothing else has. The road is still not a real road, only two sandy tire tracks. The same weeds press in on both sides. The same gray aspens and skinny pines straggle away into the distance, and the same scrubby bushes push stubbornly up from their bit of soil. Even the sounds are the same, a red squirrel clattering at me as I pass, and then a squad of blue jays squawking overhead. For a moment it's as if I had never left, as if I'm still twelve or thirteen and walking home after school.

I walk slowly, and the closer I get to the trailer, the slower I walk. The sun is dropping behind the trees. I keep looking at my watch, wondering if Father will be home. It's a workday, but what if this morning he woke up with a feeling that he should stay home? Just a feeling, he'd say to Sally. She'd go to work, though; she wouldn't want to lose the money. So when I knock on the door, it's going to be Father who'll answer. When he sees me, what will he say? Will he shout out my name? Em! Will he be amazed at how much I've grown, how I've changed? I'll remind him of the years that have passed. I'll say, Father, I've done so many things since I saw you last.

One day when I was a tiny girl, I looked up at Father and noted in astonishment how big he was. Huge! I was sure he was the tallest man with the smoothest, barest, shiniest head in the world. "My daddy," I thought, and I knew this feeling in me was love. His name was Ray Thurkill. My name was Em Thurkill. Our family was me, and Mother, whose name was Veronica Thurkill, and Father, and my sister, Pamela Thurkill. She went to school. Mother and Father went to work. Mother worked in a paper-box factory. Father worked in the gravel pits and sometimes on construction. I drew a picture of my big tall father, and another of our trailer, which was even bigger than Father.

Now I see the trailer again, and it's silly, I suppose, but I'm surprised by how small it is. Did it always list to one side that way? Looks like a pile of shit, Pamela used to say, but I never thought so. It perches on the edge of a deep ravine, like a boat waiting to sail away. Years before, the land below had been a dump, and every spring when the snow melted, ancient garbage would rise from the earth, tin cans, shards of glass, and rusted hunks of metal. I used to play down there and find pretty little pieces of pottery and try to put them together.

I walk to the front door and knock. The air is still and warm. "Hello?" I call. "Hello? Father?" I knock again, then push at the door. It swings open. And right away I see that nobody lives here anymore.

I stand in the doorway, my legs shaking, then I go in. Wads of dried leaves rustle in the corners. Porcupine pellets roll under my feet. In the room I'd shared with Pamela, mice have chewed holes in the mattress. I used to wake up bruised from Pamela's arms and legs thrashing and kicking all night long. I learned to sleep in a tiny space. Like Mother, I think.

A backless chair lies on the floor. I pick it up and open a window and poke my head out. I had made up such a nice little scene — Father at the door, crying out my name. Em! Maybe even hugging me. Then the two of us, talking about all the things that had happened in these four years. But when had we ever talked together that way?

I'd lived here for fourteen years. Here, I began to become whatever it is that makes me the person called Em. I stare down the familiar road. I'd walked that road every day for those fourteen years. I think of Mother, sad and always chilled, even in summer, and Father with his shining head, his distant eyes, and I think of Pamela, and my head begins to ache, and I lean my face against the cool window.

When I leave, the ravine is in shadow, and the sun is gone.

9

In the library downtown, I have chosen a leather chair, and I sit in it like a lady, like someone used to good things, to leather chairs and leisure. I have a magazine open in my lap, a thick magazine with smooth thick pages and every page smells good, and there are pictures of beautiful girls and boys in beautiful clothes, all of them smiling.

The leather chair has broad friendly arms, and sitting in it is like having someone else with you; it's like something alive. I can hear it breathe, and I want to pat it and say nice things to it. It creaks and breathes every time I move. It sounds like someone murmuring. I love the sound. It's the sound of being rich, of being happy and never worried. Leather is something rich people have: leather jackets and shoes, leather couches, purses, and chairs. Snakeskin and alligator leather and baby calf leather. They skin the animals and make things. Some are just babies, that's sad, but I still like this leather chair and wish I had one myself.

One of the librarians is coming toward me, and I half rise. I think he will tell me I've been here too long. He bounces past me with a smile. I sink back into the leather. This must be the best day so far. I can stay here as long as I want. Nobody cares. I can stay or go. My choice. I can think or not think. Another choice. Remember or not remember. But that's the trouble right there. I do remember, keep remembering. Remember so much I sometimes feel nauseous with it. There is the past and the present. Now and then. This and that. Pamela and Em. And then the questions. And the orders: they're all there in my head. Get a job. When are you going to look? Why aren't you working right now?

A little girl sitting on the floor nearby is looking at me. She is with another little girl, one is blonde, one dark haired. Their mouths are soft and red;

they're talking talking talking like two little women. They finger their hair, bump shoulders.

The dark one bends over, touching the toes of her red space boots. "Your boots aren't as soft as mine," she says.

"Yes, they are." The blonde frowns and touches the toes of her gray boots with tiny, pink-nailed hands.

"Your boots aren't red," the dark one accuses sweetly.

"But they're gray. Gray is good. It's good, isn't it?"

"My boots are slippery," the dark one says.

"So are mine. Slippery."

"They are not. Is your hair as soft as mine?"

"Yes, yes!"

The dark girl's hand lovingly strokes her own head. She is watching me. "My hair is much softer," she says.

"Mine is soft too," the blonde says desperately.

Are they sisters? They don't look alike, but Pamela and I didn't, either. Pamela was big, born big. She had lots of flesh. Nothing ever scared her, she did anything she wanted. She screamed at everyone, wore Father's undershirt to school and two skirts and different shoes, and if anyone asked her why she dressed like that, she stamped on their feet and said, That's why, asshole. She wouldn't comb her hair or take showers, but she loved her feet, she was vain about them, they were like Father's feet, long and slender. I always thought those feet were strange on Pamela, but they looked good on Father.

The dark girl's gaze lights on me again, and something passes over her face, something I've seen before. Her face is speaking: you can't kid me. I know what you're like, I know who you are.

I know her too. She and the blonde are the same kind. They belong to the same tribe. The better and smarter tribe. They're the ones who push aside the duds, the dupes, the dopes like me. They're the ones who know what to do, how to do it. They know what they want. How do they get that way? Are they born with that knowledge? Do they learn it somewhere? I've always felt like a stranger everywhere, unsure what to do, how to act, waiting for someone to tell me the rules. What are they? Would somebody please tell me? The dark girl knows. The blonde knows. What are they, six, maybe seven years old? — and already they know things I don't know. And they know that I don't know. And they hate me and scorn me for it. The dark one is leaning toward the blonde, their heads touch. "She's cuckoo," the dark one whispers.

"Cuckoo cuckoo," the blonde agrees.

It's high school all over, girls in the halls veering

toward me, whispering so only I can hear, "Screwed anyone lately, sweetie?"

The two little girls look at me and laugh. They whisper, whisper. One is light, one dark. Bright eyes and little pointed faces. Little wolf faces. Little wolf whispers. I remember walking the halls, my name muttering in my head against the whispers. Em-Em-Em-Em-em-em-em-mmm, the *e* disappearing, only the whining murmur of "mmmmm" in my head and the fear, the fear that that, too, would disappear.

I stand, clumsy, knocking against the chair. The little girls laugh, happy child laughter. I walk away, saying to myself that they're little girls, little little girls, only little girls.

10

Watching Oprah's show, I wish I was there with her, right there in the studio. I'm on my hands and knees, cleaning the floor and watching. I could get a mop, but you get the floor cleaner this way. This is the way Mother cleaned our floors. I have such a strong feeling that I'd like to be close to Oprah, sitting next to her and talking like a mother and a daughter. She's gotten heavy again, and she's worrying about it, but I'd tell her not to fret, I'd tell her I like her better this way. Really, I do. I'd say, You look beautiful all the time. I wish I could hug her right now and feel her solidity and tell her that. She'd hug me back and look in my face and tell me something that would help me. She's had pain and trouble, and she knows what those things are like, she knows how it is to feel sorry for yourself, to be confused and scared. I crawl over the floor, scrubbing. Oprah's strong and good, she's really good, and she hasn't forgotten other people, even though she's famous.

Every day there are ordinary people in the studio, on the stage, sitting in their chairs and telling their stories. They shout too much, they get excited and cry and yell, but Oprah says they are survivors like her. If I were on the show, I wouldn't shout: I'd be calm, I'd sit in the chair up there and talk in a low voice, pleasing. Maybe I should write her a letter, tell her if she ever does a show on sisters, I could be useful, I could tell her some things. *Just try just you try and see what happens I'll come back and kill you, kill you for once and all.*

"Shut up, Pamela. Shut up shut up." My voice is a whisper. Little voice. Tinny tiny teeny voice. Pissy scared of everything voice. I want to kill too, kill that voice, choke it, murder it out of me. I scrub harder and crawl over the floor until my knees ache.

* * *

Everyone knows your thoughts are in your brain, yet it's clear to me that my thoughts are in my stomach as well. My stomach churns with thoughts. Pamela thoughts. Father thoughts. Did-he-ever-get-my-message-about-Pamela? thoughts. Where-is-he? thoughts. Does-he-remember-he-had-two-daughters? thoughts. Does he remember? *Does* he? He still has one daughter. Does he care? I shouldn't be thinking this way. I feel bad and I'm nervous today. Nervous is when I have too many thoughts; it's like ants crawling over my skin. "Act normal," I shout at my face in the mirror. "Eat! Calm yourself with food!"

Food will make me feel better. Maybe it will. Pamela believed food could fix anything. Sad? Eat. Bruised? Eat. Sorry? Eat. She always had food with her. Bags of chips and cheese puffs on the table near her chair, her pockets stuffed with gumdrops and peppermints, peanuts and cookies, and little cream cakes in her bureau, and candy bars stashed under her pillow. They'd melt there, and she'd eat them, licking her fingers, then the paper. She especially loved one candy bar, the one with coconut filling. Whenever I wanted to get her a little something, I'd buy one of those bars.

It's Wednesday, omelette-with-onion day. I break eggs into a bowl, pour in milk, grate in cheese. This is the way Pamela must have her omelette and this is the day she must have it. Tomorrow, it will be macaroni and cheese. Friday, tomato soup and fried potatoes. Saturday, tuna-with-mayo sandwich. Oh God, there are no onions for the omelette. I check the drawer again. Above the refrigerator, Pamela's cupboard sneers at me. Private cupboard, Pamela cupboard, secret cupboard. Hinges like ears, lock a taunting mouth.

I search again: the drawer, the refrigerator, even in the oven. How can I make an onion omelette with no onions? My heart is going *tump-a tump-a tump-a*. Pamela will be furious. She will be —

No.

She will not be. Furious. Or anything. Can't be. Isn't here. Gone. Dead. I sit abruptly. I am a fool. I don't have to make an onion omelette. Not today. Not ever.

Never. Never again. And that is good, because I hate onion omelettes.

Now there's a thought for me. I. Hate. Onion. Omelettes.

I lay my head on the table, breathe into my folded arms, and think about this. I have eaten onion omelette after onion omelette after onion omelette, week upon week, month upon month, year upon year. I have eaten so many onion omelettes and always on Wednesday. And now it's Wednesday again, and I think this thought, which is not actually a new thought, but which is a thought I have not let myself consider before this.

And now another thought occurs to me, equally a revelation. I can eat anything I want for lunch. A can of potato sticks. A loaf of bread smeared with jelly. A quart of ice cream. That is what I want. Ice cream. Cold, smooth, lovely ice cream.

I open the freezer, take out the carton, get a spoon and, standing right there, begin eating. The cold slides down my throat, throbs in my temples. *Ice cream for lunch moron this is Wednesday I will kill you.* I go on eating, eating ice cream, even though it's Wednesday. I go on standing there, eating and holding the container against my belly, cooling cooling cooling my thoughts.

PART II

In the Reign of Pamela

Once, when I was sick and had to stay home alone, I found a shoe box in the back of Mother's closet. In it were all the notes that our teachers had written through the years about Pamela and me and sent home to Mother. I read the ones about myself first. "Em cries easily," my second-grade teacher wrote, "but is an eager student and loves to read. . . ." "Shy, but never a problem," my fourth-grade teacher said, "a good child."

No one wrote that Pamela was a good child,

although Mr. Emberly, a teacher Pamela had liked in sixth grade, commented that she was trying to control herself, which I knew meant cutting down on the farting and whistling, on the foot tapping and muttering. It was true that if Pamela liked a teacher, she would do homework for that teacher, she would even pass a test for that teacher. And then Mother would get a note like Mr. Emberly's. "Pamela is really trying this term!" But that was unusual. Most of the notes had an uneasy tone. "Pamela can certainly amuse her classmates if she wants to, but she's sometimes way out of control. . . ." ". . . has a wit, but her temper really gets in her way. . . ." ". . . she sometimes makes me think of a planet rocketing along in a parallel universe."

The phrase *parallel universe* slipped into my mind. I read that note four years after it was written, when I myself was in sixth grade. By then, Pamela was in high school and fighting to quit, raging that she hated everyone in the damn school and they hated her and she wanted out.

"Out! Out, out!" she screamed one night, pacing through the rooms.

"Just graduate, Pamela," Mother begged. "Only two more years to go, you won't be sorry."

Buried in the armchair, I shrank back as Pamela shouted and kicked the walls until they shook. The same way I'd chanted *happy home* as a child, I droned now, under my breath, "parallel universe parallel universe parallel universe..." The image of Pamela rolled up around herself and, like a star or a planet, burning through space, absorbed me and removed me, took me away from the storm she created. And when, suddenly, she sat down, knee to knee with Mother, and in a furious, almost pleading, tone barked into Mother's face — "All right, you win! Damn, you win. I'll do it, but only because you're making me!" — I understood that she was trying to be better, she was really trying at this moment to be good, but that, like the burning star, she was helpless to change her course.

Every morning Mother rose early to drive into the city to her job at the paper-box factory. Weekends, she shopped and cooked for the freezer and did the laundry. She was rarely still, and I thought nothing of it. That was the way it was, and I didn't know any other way, until one day I went home with Lois Merkin.

I was ten then, and astonished by Lois's tall mother, who didn't work, and whose cheeks were red and tight with health. I was even more astonished by the shining beauty of her house. Maybe I had known that such mothers and such houses existed, but if so, I had known the way you "know" what you have seen in a store window you hurry past. Yes, those exquisite mannequins, that beautiful dress, that waterfall of decorative silver foil — all are present in the world, but not in the real world, your world.

In the house, there were pictures on the walls and neat stacks of magazines on little tables. Shining green plants wreathed every window, and the furniture glowed and smelled of delicious lemon oil. I wrapped my fingers together to discipline them against their need to touch and caress each satiny surface. I left in a state of frantic greed to be invited back, and I was, and each time it was an astonishment.

How it happened that Lois and I were friends was the first astonishment. She had sought me out in school. She sat with me at lunch and told me about herself. She was going to be a missionary and save souls. Her blue eyes ignited, and enthralled by them and her clear voice and even more by the amazing fact that she knew her future, I said I would do as she did. I would be a missionary too.

"You will?" she said.

"Yes."

"Really, honestly, truly?"

"Yes."

"Swear?"

"Swear," I said passionately.

We linked pinkies. "Now you can be my friend," Lois said.

For two weeks, I went to her house every day after school. We had a snack in the large, clean kitchen, taking food from the refrigerator, which hummed powerfully and offered up such delicacies as barbecued chicken legs and cinnamon raisin bread. Then we went upstairs to her room, where Lois talked about her ballet lessons, her clothes, and how she would go to missionary college when she was seventeen.

"Yes, oh yes, oh wow," I said to everything, smiling, dazzled, in love. We would lie on her bed, hug each other, kiss, vow to always be friends and save souls together. One day we unbuttoned our blouses and looked at each other. Lois touched my nipples.

"Now do it to me," she said. She lay back with her tiny chest exposed. "You can touch them again if you want to," she said, generously. I wanted to, and that night, on my knees, I prayed for our friendship never to end.

Toward the end of the second week, Lois said it was unfair that I didn't invite her to my house. "My father says everything should be equal when you're friends. We should go to your house today. My mother said it was okay."

We took the school bus and got off at the Corners.

Going down our road, I walked as slowly as possible. Maybe Pamela wouldn't be home. Maybe if she was, she wouldn't say anything wrong. Maybe she would like Lois and be nice. Our home came into view.

"I feel so sorry for the people who live there," Lois said.

I looked at the trailer, seeing what she saw: a long, narrow, rusty tin can sitting on concrete blocks. I walked toward the door. "Where're you going?" she said. In the kitchen, I wiped the table and took a box of gingersnaps from the cupboard. Lois edged in slowly. "You live here?"

I put milk and two glasses on the table. "You can sit down."

She bit into a cookie with her tiny teeth. Her eyes flashed from corner to corner. "Where's your mother?"

"Working. You want to see my room?"

She nodded, but Pamela came in then, banging the door. "Who's this?" she said, chewing on her lip, and I knew that everything was lost. Her hair was yellow and tangled, her eyes alight with the pleasure of what she was about to do. "Who's this weird-looking person, Em? Who's this pale piggy ghosty girl?"

"This is Lois."

"LO-kiss?" She leaned over the table. "What's the matter with you, little LO-kiss?" Pamela hung her tongue out of her mouth, playing the idiot. "Why don't you say something? You got a little poker stuck up your little BEE-hind?"

"We're going to my room, Pamela."

"Your room?" Pamela dipped her finger into Lois's milk, licked it, and dipped it in again. "That's my room, turdface, and you don't go in there unless I say so. Right, LO-kiss my ass?"

"You should have your mouth washed out with soap," Lois managed to say.

"And you should have your mouth washed out with raccoon crap," Pamela said. "I got a nice fresh lump of it right here in the fridge." She opened the refrigerator. "You want some?"

Lois went out the door and I went after her. We walked to the grocery store at the Corners, where she called her father to come get her. "My sister was in a bad mood today," I said.

Lois stared up the road. "You don't have to wait with me."

"She's okay most of the time."

A car appeared around the bend and Lois let out a scream. "Daddy!"

"She really is mostly okay," I said again. "Really!"

Lois ran and got into the car. I stepped to the side of the road, and as they passed I waved my arm and called, "Bye! Bye, Lois! See you in school tomorrow!"

12

Friday was payday. Father always went out for beer and came home, as Mother said, "late, foolish, and sleepy." Every so often, though, he would drink straight through the night, and then Mother would wake us, whispering into our faces, "Girls, girls, wake up. Wake up, go hide." And the next day, putting ice on her bruises, she would murmur apologetically, "He didn't mean it. He just got out of hand."

Hiding behind a chair or crouching under the table, I would stare, fascinated and horrified, at

Father's hands. They were brown and long, slender, hard, sinewy, like all of him. If he got out of hand, then he must have been "in hand" to begin with. In his own hand. How was this possible? In the mysterious way of adults, he had managed an amazing feat! Held himself in his own hand! And then jumped out and maybe hurt himself and got mad? And was that why he hurt Mother? I wished he would never get "out of hand" again. And for a long time, for months at a stretch, he wouldn't. Later, when I was older, I heard Mother say, "The drink has him," and I understood and thought, Poor Father.

But on those nights when Mother woke us, there was no understanding, no thinking, only something thick and suffocating, crowding my throat. Only running, and bare feet pounding, sweaty hands, and the slap of night air on my face. Sometimes Pamela led me into the woods, where we pressed against the trees and she told me to shut up shut up and stop crying or else. And sometimes we crawled under the trailer where, lying with my face pressed into the iron-smelling earth — Mother's cries in one ear, Pamela's curses in the other — I counted backward, recited rhymes, and told myself stories as the hours passed.

In the morning, when we went back into the house, filthy and dazed with fatigue, Father would be at the table, drinking coffee. "You girls," he'd say, hanging his head. And then, with a smile so sad it broke my heart, "I'm sorry, you girls. I'm sorry."

All day Mother would stay in bed and Father would shuffle around the house, making cups of tea for her, and telling us he was going to buy us presents of all kinds. Dolls and dresses, games and shoes. Pamela would make the arm-chopping sign and say Sure, sure, he'd do it when the sun turned to horseballs.

But once he did bring us something, a chocolate cake with tiny silver dots decorating the stiff white frosting. He put it in the middle of the table and said, "Dig in, girls." We ate chunk after chunk of the sweet soft crumbly cake, while he sat there, watching us. "Veronica!" he called Mother. "Come look at this, look at these girls of yours. It's my birthday today, and they're eating all my cake."

"Your birthday!" My mouth fell open.

"Are you little pigs going to leave me a bite of my own cake?"

Mother giggled, passing her hand over her mouth. Then I laughed, and Pamela laughed. We all laughed at Father's joke. We were all laughing together, like a real family.

13

The winter I was thirteen, Mother had a cold, a flu, a virus, a bug. Every day she called it something else. She had headaches and a little fever all the time. She said her legs were weak, and her head felt as if someone were sticking heavy pins in it. Day after day, the sky was gray and snow fell, thick thick snow. It piled up on the roof, in the trees, on the sides of the road. Then the snow stopped and the temperature fell, and each day was colder than the day before.

Mother shivered and held her elbows. Her fever

was worse at night. She said sometimes thoughts entered her head that she didn't understand. "It's like I'm dreaming, but awake. All these dreams, it's so strange, I don't know what to think of it." One day she said, "At work today, I felt like I was already dead."

"But you feel better now?" I said. "You feel better now, don't you? You don't feel that way now, do you?"

"Maybe in the morning I'll feel better," she said.

She had always gotten up in the morning and gone to work, no matter what; but now, sometimes she stayed home and rested. One morning I heard her in the bathroom, vomiting. "Maybe I should go to the doctor," she said. She held the wall to steady herself and went back to bed.

She was still there when I came in from school. I asked if she wanted something to eat. She shook her head. It was Friday. I toasted waffles for supper. Pamela opened one of Father's beers. He was still not home when I went to bed, but in the morning he was on the couch, asleep, his long legs trailing over the arm. Mother was quiet in her room. She didn't answer when I opened the door and asked if she wanted breakfast.

At noon, I knocked on her door and went in. She was lying under the heaped blankets. I bent over her and called her. She wouldn't open her eyes. "Mother."

I shook her by the shoulder. "Mother, wake up." I kept shaking her and saying this.

I think I had known from the moment I stepped into the room that she was gone, but my mind whispered to me that if I didn't agree to it, it might not be true. "Mother," I said. I spoke reasonably. "Mother, wake up." Something lodged itself between my eyes, something small and hard. It tapped at my brain like a tiny persistent hammer. "Please, Mother," I said, "please wake up." I wanted to be standing at her door again, to be in that place where I could pretend she would still answer me.

The doctor who signed the death certificate said it was probably a heart attack, but some time later we were told it was a rare infection of the heart. Her body was taken away. I stood at the window and watched them load the stretcher into the back of the ambulance. It seemed strange to me that they would take her to the hospital, now that she was dead.

Father said he would not cremate her, though it was cheaper. There was a place in Highbridge Cemetery where his mother was buried. There was room there for Mother, he said, "and me, when I go." Pamela refused to go to the funeral. "I'm not watching them put Ma in a hole in the ground," she said, so it was Father and me only. Father cried, his bony shoulders curved around himself, his long smooth head turning purple in the cold. My own head seemed large for my body, light and fragile, like a blown-up paper balloon. I couldn't cry.

At home, Father gathered Mother's clothes and her bits of makeup and jewelry, some necklaces of colored stones, a few earrings. I watched him move through their room, stuffing her things into grocery bags. He loaded them into the backseat of his car. "What are you doing?" I said.

"Going to the dump." He got behind the wheel.

I reached into one of the bags and pulled out Mother's green sweater, the one with the cat buttons. "What do you want that for?" he said.

"I don't know." I held the sweater against myself.

He shook his head. "Em, child, it'll only make you feel worse."

"I want it."

"Suit yourself."

I wore the sweater for weeks. I didn't take it off, except to bathe. I drifted from room to room, not knowing where the hours went. I stood in front of her window, looking at the gray sky and the black trees and the banks of snow lining the road. Sometimes I sat in her chair, drinking a boiling cup of black tea the way she did at the end of a day. Sometimes I lay down and slept. But even awake I felt as if I were sleeping.

At night I dreamed about her: she was calling me to come scratch her back, she was asking if I'd remembered to eat breakfast.

My heart then seemed to be located in the throbbing center of my forehead, or else deep in my throat. I was aware of its weight, and it seemed both as heavy as stone and as fragile as a walnut, which could be cracked with a single rap of the hand. Inside were the two halves of myself, like the two halves of my heart; in one half lay guilt, in the other grief, and each had an equal claim on me. I wondered why I had not been better to her, more considerate, more loving, why I had never kissed her more, as now I longed to do, a thousand kisses for her cheeks, another thousand for each hand. Why hadn't I told her every single day of her life that I loved her? Why hadn't I wrapped her green sweater more closely about her shoulders when she couldn't get warm, and brought her a scarf for her throat, which was always raw, which was always "troubling" her?

Every day I was newly distressed with these thoughts, freshly surprised by her absence. She had been small, she had hardly taken up any room, but without her, how empty the trailer was, how quiet, large, and chilly. I held my elbows and waited for her to come back: waited for the door to open, for her to walk in, coughing and telling me to be a good girl.

14

Evening after evening, Father sat on the couch, elbows on his knees, staring blankly at the TV. His narrow face, his hands veined and rough, his skinny, hard body, all filled me with pity. In his eyes there was a hot, stunned look. He seemed listless, yet ready for action — as if, at any moment, he might burst out of his skin and explode through the roof, leaving us as Mother had.

Pamela didn't go back to school, and Father said she should get a job. She went to work in a potato-chip factory. Then a laundry. Then the box factory, where Mother had worked. She was fired from each job, and after the box factory, she refused to look for work again. She said she would take care of the house, do the things Mother had done. Laundry piled up, the windows were streaked with bird goo. Wrapped in a frayed blue quilt, Pamela lay on the couch watching TV – rising, it seemed, only to pee or open another can of potato sticks. Sometimes she cooked supper for us, sometimes not. I could always find something to eat, toast or tuna fish, but Father said a workingman had to have a decent meal at the end of a hard day.

"You don't give me enough money for food," Pamela said.

Father said he certainly did. "Same thing I gave your mother. Same thing. And look at the meals we ate then."

"I know what you gave her," Pamela said. "You gave her shit, that's all you ever gave her. I don't want you to even talk about her."

Father's face was the color of clay. "Don't you go telling me who to talk about," he said.

"I'll tell you anything I damn want." Pamela stood up, the quilt heaving around her shoulders. She was nearly as tall as Father and must have weighed almost as much. "It's your fault she's dead."

Father chewed his lip, as if he were going to bite

it off. He gave Pamela a single terrible look and slammed out. We heard the car motor and the tires spinning.

"I wish you weren't so mean to Father," I said.

She whirled and slapped me in the face. "Who's mean? You don't know what you're talking about!" She slapped me again.

"Pamela!" I ran into our room, my hands over my face.

"Wake up!" she shouted after me. "You're always looking asleep these days. I hate that sleeping look!"

Her handprint was still on my face in the morning, and I didn't go to school that day.

One Friday, Pamela yelled for me to come outside with her. She was wearing jeans, a plaid shirt, and an old hunting jacket of Father's. The cold had lifted, and filthy mounds of melting snow were everywhere. "What are we doing?" I said.

Pamela got behind the wheel of Mother's car. "You'll see." She patted my knee. "Just watch this, little sis."

She didn't have a license. She'd learned to drive, she said, by watching Mother, but Mother had never handled her car as if it were a bucking horse she was taming by sheer physical force. We barreled down the road. Pamela wrenched the wheel one way, then the other, slammed on the brakes at intersections, and pounded the gas pedal. We couldn't stop laughing. It was almost like being with the kind of big sister I read about in my books.

At the gravel works, Pamela parked by the gate. When the men started coming through, we got out of the car to look for Father. "There he is," Pamela said. He was in a cluster of men carrying lunch pails. Pamela walked up to him. "Give me your pay envelope," she said.

The men looked at her, then at Father, and they laughed.

"Go home," Father said. "What do you want? Go home, Em," he said to me. "You don't belong here."

"Don't talk to us like we're dogs," Pamela said. "I want money for food, and not you drinking it all up."

"She's got your number, Ray," one of the men said. They laughed harder.

Father thrust money into Pamela's hand. "More," she said. He gave her another bill, and we left.

Every Friday after that, we went to meet him. If he didn't give her as much money as she wanted, Pamela gripped my arm and squeezed until I could barely stand it. "Cry, you little bitch!" she urged.

I moaned and twisted, but I didn't cry. I wouldn't let myself. Bad enough that she called out to the people in the parking lot to look at me, to feel sorry for me.

"My little sister is going hungry, because our

excuse for a father is drinking up his check. Look at this poor kid, everyone! Look at my father — look at him right here!"

She always got more money, but we didn't eat any better, and Father said she must be hiding it. "You've got a wad somewhere," he said. "I know you, Pamela. You've got it sneaked away."

"You think so?" she said. "Where would that be?"

"You tell me. You got it somewhere. I know you," he said again.

"He knows me," she said. "He knows me!" She was excited: she liked fighting with Father. She liked it when he went searching for the money, digging into drawers and closets, looking under our mattress, and even checking the freezer and the oven. "Look — look all you want," she said. "You'll never find it. Because — "

"Because what?" He stood with his hands on his hips. His skull reddened.

"Because I say so. Because there ain't any wad. Because you'll never find where I hid it. If I hid it. If," she said. "If, if, if," she shouted. "If, if, if, if, if!"

I went outside and sat in Mother's car, parked under an oak tree on the bank of the creek. I could still hear Pamela shouting, "If, if, if, if —"

"If 'ifs' and 'ands' were pots and pans, we'd all be tinkers," I sang, and then sang it again. It was one of

Mother's sayings. I liked it. I liked repeating the things she'd said. I leaned my head back to look at the sky. "If 'ifs' and 'ands' were pots and pans, we'd all be tinkers." The waxing moon, shining through the trees, seemed to be calmly waiting for me to say something else.

"I waited for you," Frank August said.

I nodded. The buses were gone, the parking lot and school were deserted. I sat on the back steps with him. I didn't want to go home. At home, there was Father, morose, slumped, sniffling tears up his nose or fighting with Pamela. And there was the mess and the bad smell of the trailer, the staleness and disorder, and Pamela wrapped in the blue quilt.

Frank August had heavy, sleepy-looking eyes. Bedroom eyes, they were called. He drew me toward him, touched me through my blouse, walked his hand like silk under my skirt. "Yes?" he said. "Yesss?"

I didn't say anything. I didn't move or speak. I thought, How funny . . . August in May . . . I thought about being fourteen. So much older than thirteen. I thought about my birthday the month before, the first ever without Mother, and how no one had noticed. I moved closer to Frank August.

We sat there other days, and each time I thought,

August in May, and closed my eyes and heard him say Yesss? And each time there were his sleepy eyes and his hands on my skin. His lovely lovely hands.

Then he stopped waiting for me outside, but other boys came up to me. "Hey, Em, how are you?" they said. And, "Em, maybe we could go for a ride?" Some of them were the nice boys, the ones with high bright foreheads. They drove their parents' old cars and parked on back roads and told me I was pretty. "Let's do things," they said, and we did, in the car or standing against a tree. Sometimes they asked me to take off my clothes, and I did. I would fold my things neatly on the seat of the car and stand for a moment in the cool sweet air and watch their faces. Then I'd put my clothes back on. "Aw, what'd you do that for?" they said. "Aw, Em."

I didn't say anything. As long as they were nice, I let them do what they wanted, and sometimes it was so sweet — their eager voices, their hands, the way they said "Please" and "Oh, Em." And when it was that way, sweet sweet, something inside me lifted and rose, and the darkness went away for a while.

15

The summer days were long and slow. I had almost nothing to do with my time. I slept heavily and woke feeling tired. I dreamed about Mother often. One night I dreamed that Mother and I were in a railroad car, sitting at a table with a pink cloth, looking at the menu. There was a small vase with a frilled pink flower in the middle of the table.

"Mother," I said, "look how pretty all this is! Aren't you glad we got here?" It seemed there had been some trouble in our finding the right train.

"Choose anything you want," Mother said. "You can have anything, Em. You only have to say."

I felt immensely happy. I leaped over the table and wrapped my arms around her. "Are you sure?" I asked. "Are you absolutely sure?"

"Yes," she said. She said it very strongly, in a big voice, a voice she'd never had when she was alive. "Yes. I'm your mother, aren't I?"

When I woke up, the feeling of happiness was still there, and only slowly disappeared as the long hot day passed.

Sometimes I walked to the store at the Corners and stayed around there, helping out. I waited on customers or stacked things on the shelves. Sometimes I pumped gasoline and washed windshields. Mr. Miller, who owned the store, said he couldn't hire me, but now and then he would give me a five-dollar bill.

One day, a boy drove up in a red pickup. It was a Saturday in July. Day after day the weather had been hot and humid. At home we kept the windows and doors open, but the walls streamed and the floors were sticky. Sometimes it was hard to breathe.

"Hey," the boy said. "How you doing?"

"Okay."

I knew him from school. His name was Dennis Walter. He filled the gas tank. While he was inside, paying, I cleaned the windshield.

"So you work here?" he said when he came back out. He was a skinny boy with red hair and a funny nose, tilted to one side.

"Sort of."

"You working right now?"

"Sort of."

He laughed. "Yes or no?"

"No."

"You want a ride home or anything?"

"No. Thank you," I added.

"You sure?" He smiled at me.

"Well . . . okay," I said. I got in the truck and sat near the window.

"So where do you want to go?" he asked. He pulled out onto the road.

"Home. I live on Killenhorn Road."

He nodded, but at Killenhorn Road, he kept going.

"That was it," I said. "That was Killenhorn Road, where I live."

He took the next turnoff. It was a sandy road, like ours, with not quite enough room for two cars, but longer and rising in a series of twisting hills. He stopped the pickup near a farmer's field. "Em," he said.

"What?"

"You want to do something?"

I shook my head.

"Just something," he said. "Okay?"

"Like what?"

"Like, you could just take off your clothes."

"No."

"Why not?"

"I don't want to."

"Just for a minute, Em. Okay?"

"I can walk home," I said. I got out of the truck and started back down the road.

He followed me, his head out the window. "Come on, Em," he said, "come on."

I shook my head. I felt a little bit scared, but I didn't want to "do something" with him. It wasn't just him. Frank August and all those other boys were like a dream now. My bad dream. Well, not all bad, but not a good dream, either. The one I'd had about Mother was my good dream.

Scuffing down the dusty road, I remembered that dream. I remembered how Mother and I had read the menu together. If I could hold on to that memory, I thought, I wouldn't feel so lonely. I told myself the train story again. I became absorbed in it. I remembered the pink tablecloth and the happiness of leaping over it to embrace Mother. I forgot Dennis following me in the pickup.

Suddenly he yelled, "Screw you, Em!" He gunned the motor and swerved toward me as if he wanted to kill me. I screamed and jumped off the road into the ditch. The tires spit sand as he went past. I walked in the ditch for a few minutes, rubbing sand out of my eyes; then I went back up on the road and walked the rest of the way home.

16

"You just never know what's going to happen," Father said, standing in the kitchen. "Isn't that right, girls? You just never know if you're going to meet a certain person or not. You don't ever think you are, and then you do. See what I mean, girls?"

A long speech for Father.

Silence descended. Sitting next to me, big legs thrusting out of cutoffs, Pamela breathed furiously. I smelled her strong sweat. It was noon, and outside the blue jays called like creaky doors opening and closing.

Father's forehead shone with sweat; there were two dark circles under the arms of his green work shirt. But standing next to him, her hip slouched against his, Sally Pearson was cool. She was cool in a white, short-sleeved blouse and tight-fitting white jeans. She and Father held hands as if they were in high school, as if they were just a couple of kids, while Pamela and I sat at the kitchen table like grown-ups, or a pair of sour judges. We sat there unspeaking, our arms folded, as if we were adults passing judgment on our wayward children.

"Sally works in the office of the gravel company," Father said. "That's where we met." He smiled. Such a rare thing, Father's smile. And this smile! A boy's smile, a boy's large smile of innocent delight. It was as if, overnight, he had become someone else entirely, no longer our silent, miserable father.

"I do the paychecks," Sally said. She smiled too, but it was different. A cool, silver smile. She was nearly as tall as Father, and she had gray hair, as if she were old like him, but that was different too. Her hair was long and shining, and anyone could see that she wasn't much older than Pamela.

"So what do you say, Em?" she said. "Pamela, what about you? You can't fool me — I know what you're thinking." She looked at Father and laughed. "Your girls don't like me, Ray."

"Sure they do," he said.

"You do the paychecks?" Pamela said, breaking our silence. She blew her nose on her sleeve. "What do you do with them, shove them up your ass?"

"Pamela," Father said. "Pamela, be nice! Don't pay her no attention," he said to Sally. "She don't mean it."

"You're too sweet," Sally said to him. And then, to us, "I always liked your father. And lately, we got talking and stuff, but this isn't any fast thing. We've known each other a long time."

Pamela spit on the table. The glob of spit, yellowish and thick, quivered like it was alive. "So what are you doing here?" she said. "What do you want?"

"We got married," Father said.

"Yesterday," Sally said. She smiled, eyeing Pamela.

Pamela stood up, knocking over her chair. "You lie! Both of you, you're two liars."

"Are we?" Sally held out her hand. She wore a gold wedding ring. And Father took the marriage certificate out of an envelope and laid it on the table for us to see.

Sally moved her things into Father and Mother's room that afternoon. And later that same day, Father said we should call her "Mother."

"Afungoola!" Pamela shouted, a curse she had

picked up in her brief working career. "I'll call her what I want to call her, and you know what that is? *Nothing.*"

In our room, she told me she would never call Sally "Mother," she would not even speak to her, and I had better not, either, if I knew what was good for me.

"I wouldn't," I said. "Do you think I would?" I spit out the window to show her how I felt, but my spit was pale and thin.

Sally didn't like our furniture. She got rid of the old couch first. "Who the hell said she could do that?" Pamela demanded of Father.

"It's her house now," Father said.

The easy chair went next, then the rugs and the bed that Mother and Father had shared. As fast as the old things went out, the new came in. Sally gave away sheets, towels, pillows. She packed up the dishes we'd always used — pale yellow with faded little flowers around the borders — and said the Salvation Army was the place for them. The new dishes were a complete set in two colors, hot pink and bright green, with a matching gravy boat, creamer, and sugar bowl. She put up pictures on the walls of barns and little girls with big eyes, changed the toothbrush holder in the bathroom, and lined the windowsills with silk African violets. "Don't they just look so real, Em?" she said.

She talked to me all the time and never waited for an answer. She sent out words as if they were packages she was tossing on my porch as she passed and didn't care whether I opened them or not. I knew she wasn't afraid of me, the way she was of Pamela. They hated each other. When they were in the same room, something else was there too, taking up air and space: as if hate were solid, as if it had substance and a shape.

Weekends were the hardest time. Sally and Father were home then, touching and bumping into each other, and murmuring as if they had a thousand little secrets. Nothing was the same anymore: not Father, not the furniture, not any of us. Only Pamela sometimes seemed unchanged, but even that wasn't true. Without Mother, she was Pamela intensified, the rocketing planet, the exploding star in free fall. She did and said anything she wanted, and no one stopped her. No one could.

Sometimes, just to get away from them all — to be by myself — I went out back and sat in Mother's car. It still smelled like Smith Brothers Wild Cherry Cough Drops, Mother's favorite. If only I could drive, I thought. If only Mother were still alive. If only I had been good all the time, and not just sometimes.

One day, Father got in next to me. "Hello, Em."

"Hello, Father."

Then he just sat there. "It's quiet here," he said at last. There was another silence. He twisted the new gold ring on his left hand. "Well, I just thought — I came out here so maybe we could talk."

"Okay," I said.

"You like to play here?" He took a blue handkerchief from his back pocket and wiped his face.

"I don't play."

"What do you do?"

"Nothing." Could I tell him I made up stories? That I pretended? That I thought about *someday*? Someday, when I was grown up. When I was in college. When I was someone different than I was now.

"So you just sit out here?"

"Yes. I guess so." I let my hand slide across the gray plush seat. It was worn, bare in spots, but I loved the soft feel of it, and the way Mother's smell was in it.

"Well, I just thought —" He folded the handkerchief and put it back into his pocket. "You know — Sally, she's someone good. I mean, I know she's not your mother, but she's good. Your sister, she's pretty hard on Sally. Maybe you could talk to her."

"Maybe," I said.

"Look at this, Em." He held out his hand, showing me his wedding band, gleaming gold. "She bought it for me," he said. "Isn't that something? And, I'll tell you something else, do you see me drinking now? No, you don't. I promised her I wouldn't, and I don't."

I stared out the windshield. *You didn't do that for Mother.* I dug my hands deep into the pockets of my green jacket. It was November already and cold in the car. I wanted him to go away. I had not hated him so much in a long time.

"She's like a birthday present," he said. "A pretty big surprise for me. Well, that's all I got to say. I just thought, you know, if you could think about that." He opened the door and left.

A few days later, Sally told me she had decided to take Mother's car for herself. "No use letting it go to waste," she said. "Perfectly good car — it should be used. Agree, Em?"

It was another question to which she didn't expect an answer. She took Mother's car to a mechanic for an overhaul and when that was done she had it repainted. It had been a faded black for as long as I could remember. When she brought it home, it was vivid red, with new red-and-green-plaid seat covers and a leather wheel cover. She drove it everywhere and, one day, when she took me into town to help her with the shopping, I realized that the car no longer even smelled like Mother.

17

Just before Thanksgiving, Sally told Pamela and me that we had to get jobs and pay her and Father room and board if we wanted to go on living with them. "What about school?" I said.

"What about it?" she said. "What's the problem?"

"How can I work? I go to school."

"You ever hear of part-time? Not you," she said to Pamela. "Full-time for you. I'm sick of you slopping around the house without doing one tiny productive thing for this family."

"You are really messed," Pamela said. "You think I'm going to work and then give you the money?"

"Yeah, that's just what I think," Sally said. "Or else you don't get to eat. Same for you, Em," she said. "Don't give me that pathetic look. What are you, sixteen?"

"Fourteen. In April, I'll be fifteen."

"Okay, so the April after that, you'll be sixteen and through with school."

"What?" There was a smile on my face. I didn't want it there, but I couldn't take it off.

"You heard me. What do you think, you can stay in school forever? Look, get yourself a part-time job. After school, before school, I don't care. I went to work when I was twelve, so what makes you special? Bring something into the household. Get used to it: your dad isn't going to support you the rest of your life."

18

Pamela fanned a wad of twenty- and fifty-dollar bills in front of me. "Remember how he tore up the place looking for this?"

"You mean Father?" I said. I had never seen so much money at once.

"You mean Faaa-ther," she mimicked. "Yes, I mean Faaa-ther."

She'd had the money all this time, she said, hidden away in a tin box under the trailer. "Our old hidey-hole," she said, triumphant. She caressed the bills.

"But what are you going to do with it?" I said.

"Sometimes you are so so so stupid. We're going to leave."

"What?"

"You having trouble with your hearing?"

"Leave here? Why?"

She looked me level in the eye. "It's either that, or I kill that bitch."

We left one morning after Father and Sally had gone to work. We packed two suitcases with clothes and walked to the Corners, where we took a bus into the city.

"We didn't even say good-bye to him," I said. I looked out the window and thought of Father and how, that day in the car, he had wiped his face with the blue handkerchief and looked at me so pleadingly, as if he thought he could get me to love Sally too.

In the city, everything was different. The smell of the air and the way people dressed and talked and even how they walked. And there were so many people. They were everywhere. I stood outside the bus station with my suitcase, and I didn't know which way to look first, or if we should go forward or back, cross the street or stay right there.

Pamela said we had to buy a newspaper and read

the FOR RENT ads. So we did that. And then we called a few places and saw some apartments. She wasn't used to walking around so much and climbing stairs, and she got cranky. We went back to the first place we'd seen, a room in an old brick building near the college. Pamela said she'd be damned if she'd live near a bunch of snotty college kids, but the apartment was on the ground floor and the landlady had said there was a mattress in the basement that we could use.

"Thurkill?" the landlady said. "That's a funny name." Her own name was Blossom Smith. "Thurkill?" she repeated. "What is that?"

"It's our damn name," Pamela said. "Anything else you want to know?"

Blossom Smith took a fresh cigarette from a pack stuck in her rolled-up shirtsleeve. "Going to school, are you, girls?" She looked at me closely.

"Maybe," I managed to say.

"How old are you?"

"Seventeen." My heart pounded at the lie.

Blossom Smith grimaced. "You look young for your age." She had dyed black hair and smoked her cigarette from the corner of her mouth. "So where're you from?" She unlocked the door to the room. The only thing in it was a lamp with a paper shade, plugged into a wall socket. "I can tell you're not city girls."

Pamela went to one of the windows and snapped up the shade. She hated answering questions. "These are real cheap," she said. "They're going to tear in a minute."

"We can pay the first month's rent right now," I said quickly. "Can't we, Pamela?"

She opened her wallet and slowly counted bills into Blossom Smith's hand. Blossom Smith counted the bills again, then folded them up and tucked them into a front pocket of her jeans.

After she left, Pamela sat down on her suitcase. "Shit, I'm beat."

"Me too."

"I don't want to do anything."

"Me neither."

"Just call a restaurant and send over the food."

"Yeah!"

We looked at each other and laughed.

Later, we dragged the mattress up from the basement. It smelled like cat pee, and I didn't want to sleep on it. We covered it with a sheet. "I don't smell anything anymore," Pamela said.

"I still do."

"No you don't."

"Yes I do, Pamela."

"Shut up! Get your nose in your armpit." She

laughed. "Smells sweet as roses, don't it?" she said. She pulled her sweater over her and fell asleep.

A few days later we found a good mattress in a secondhand store called the Bargain Shop. Pamela loved that place. Every day we bought something else for our room: a bureau, a table, a chair, even a wall plaque showing geese in flight over trees. "Our little home," Pamela said, the day I hammered the plaque into the wall over her bed.

It was a friendly time between us, almost happy. Evenings, when we pulled the shades and the lamps threw shadows against the walls, I was intensely aware that here we were, the two of us together in our little room — and outside was the rest of the world, strangers all.

December passed, and January. There were always things to do, shopping and fixing meals and taking out books from the library. I missed school, but Pamela said that if I enrolled now, Sally could find out where we were and make us come back and work for her.

I didn't think much about money. Pamela was in charge of that. She doled it out from her wallet and checked every receipt to make sure no one cheated us. It seemed as if the supply of money would never run out. Then one morning in February, there was a knock on the door. "Sheriff's office," a man called. "Please open." Three men came in and carried our things out to the curb, everything except the smelly cat mattress. Pamela hadn't paid the rent for two months, and Blossom Smith had an eviction order from the sheriff's department.

19

Pamela cursed Blossom Smith, and the men who carried out our stuff, and the sheriff, and every passer-by. We were sitting on the curb with all our things — the furniture and bags and boxes of clothes and kitchenware — tumbled behind us in the dirty snow.

"We have to do something," I said.

"Well, do it then." She put her head on her knees and pretended to sleep.

"Pamela." I shook her shoulder. "What do you want me to do?"

She turned her face and looked up at me. "Can't you figure anything out? You are so stupid, it's disgusting." A small line of snot came out of her left nostril.

I thought about walking to the corner and turning that corner and walking on and not coming back, ever. Just take care of myself. Let Pamela take care of herself.

"Your nose," I said.

"What about it?"

"It's snotty."

She laughed and wiped her nose across the sleeve of her jacket. "Better?"

"Yeah."

After a while I got up and went down the street to a medical building. There was a pay phone in the lobby that I'd used before. I called a storage company. They came about two hours later and took our stuff away.

That night we slept in the bus station. In the morning the temperature was below zero outside, so we stayed there. We used the bathroom to clean up, and ate other people's leftover food. We slept there two more nights, dozing in the hard plastic bucket seats with their tiny attached TVs. Sometime in the middle of the third night, I woke to see the bearded face of a man looming over me. "It's okay, don't get scared," he said. There was a woman with him.

"Don't you want to sleep someplace warmer," she said, "on a real bed?"

"Your sister seems to have some emotional problems," the social worker in the shelter said. "How long has she been like this?"

"Like what?" I didn't know if I liked Mr. Elias. I knew I didn't like his questions.

"Well, take her language, for instance. It's, uh, pretty coarse. And her body language — negative body language." Mr. Elias shook his head. He was a little man with a hard potbelly that pressed against the desk. "And I might as well add the way she dresses — something wrong with that. All those clothes."

"She gets cold," I said. For a moment, he looked as if he might believe me. In the last month or so, Pamela had taken to wearing layers of skirts, multiple sweaters and shawls, two hats or three, and painting her cheeks with bright round circles of red.

"It's her *affect*," he said. "The whole package. Affect means the overall impression she gives," he lectured. "You understand? She gives an impression of being strong, but there's something off-key there. Does she have a history of emotional disturbance?"

I knew I should answer his questions, but I didn't want to. There was something about this that bothered me, scared me. Yes, Pamela was a little peculiar, but so what? That was the way she was.

"Were there any incidents in your family with your sister?" His hand, with a pen in it, was poised over a yellow legal pad.

Something kept me from speaking. Was it pride? Mother wouldn't like me talking about family problems, nor would Father. But maybe it was just fear that they could take Pamela away and lock her up, and me with her.

"Your affect, on the other hand," he said, putting down his pen, "is the opposite of your sister. Pleasant, a bit timid."

"Timid," I repeated. I didn't like that, either.

We had been in the shelter for over a week. We slept on cots in a room with a dozen other women. Some of them cried, some of them smelled, some of them tried to talk to us. "Don't you talk to anyone," Pamela warned me. She clutched my arm. "They're all crazy in here." Every morning we folded the stiff green blankets at the foot of the beds and then washed in the crowded bathroom, before we got breakfast. Every day we had to leave the shelter and stay away until the evening meal. The weather was cold and we discovered different places where we could sit without being bothered. The library was good, and so was the ladies' lounge in one of the big department stores. If we had money — mostly we didn't, but once we found a ten-dollar bill while we were crossing the street, and a few times we begged — we bought food and ate it there. The doors on the stalls creaked open and shut, open and shut, and the toilets flushed, but it was warm.

When Mr. Elias asked my age, I told him seventeen. I sat up straight and said it without expression.

"You're small for your age," he said.

"Like my mother." I wound my hands together in my lap.

"Where is your mother?"

"Dead."

"And your father?"

I hesitated, then said, "Dead." It was true, in a way, wasn't it?

"So it's just you and your sister?"

"Yes."

"I'm sorry," he said. He leaned across the desk. "It must be hard. Are you scared of Pamela?"

"Scared? No."

"You have no difficulty dealing with her?"

I shook my head.

"You're devoted to her."

"She's my sister."

He sat there, looking at me. Was he thinking about my "affect"? I wondered how long we could go on staying here, and how we were going to live when we left. Crazy Pamela. Timid me.

"What are your plans?" he asked.

"I don't know."

"Have you looked for work?"

I shook my head.

"What about your sister? Can she hold down a job?"

I shrugged. "She gets fired. She fights with people."

"Ah," he said, as if he weren't surprised. "She might qualify for a disability check. But you need to find a job."

"Okay." I wondered what I could do, and who would even want to hire me.

Mr. Elias arranged for Pamela to have two interviews with a psychologist. After the first one, she was in a fury. "You hear those idiot questions he asked me? All he wanted was to get in my brain and mess it up. That little turd, he wanted me to draw pictures for him. Fruck I will!" She pinched me hard. "And you love it, you and Elias, you two billing and cooing together, you love me going there."

I rubbed my arm. "Pamela, you got it wrong." We were in the ladies' lounge in the department store. "I told you, Mr. Elias said if you go to the interviews, maybe you could get a check every month. Remember? It wouldn't be much, he said, but it would be someth —"

"Don't tell me again what frucking Feelius said! He's another moron. I'm not going back!" Her cheeks had a raw flush, and she slapped me.

"Fine," I managed to say. I didn't cry. I never did when she hit or pinched me, but sometimes the effort seemed to drive the tears back into my head like nails. I went to the watercooler and drank. "We'll just go on staying in the shelter forever."

She smirked, as if I'd finally said something sensible, but the following week she went to the second appointment.

20

"You have to project confidence when you're looking for work, Em," Mr. Elias said.

"Yes," I said.

"You have to speak up."

"Yes."

"Sometimes you whisper. Like now, I can hardly hear you. I want you to use a big voice. All right?"

"All right."

"Louder!"

"All right."

"Good. And smile. Like that. That's right. You have a nice smile."

The first place I tried was the department store where Pamela and I had waited out hours in the ladies' lounge. I filled out an application, then sat on a bench outside the personnel office. A parade of people with important-looking folders under their arms rushed in and out. An hour passed before I was called. A man wearing a white shirt and a blue bow tie sat behind a desk.

"Yes, what can I do for you?" he said without looking at me.

"I'm . . . looking for work." It came out in a whisper.

He held out his hand for my application. "Do you have any experience as a salesperson?"

"No."

"What can you do?"

"Anything you want me to."

He looked up and almost smiled. "I don't have anything now. Try me again in a month."

I went to the next place. And the next. And then another place. And the next day I did the same thing.

And the day after that. Every day I walked in and out of offices, shops, and factories, as if on a treadmill or in a dream. At night, under the green blanket, my dreams were crowded with offices and applications and voices asking me questions. Can you use a computer? Are you willing to work Saturdays? How old are you? Do you have any experience? How long were you on your last job?

In the dreams and in life, I filled in each line of the endless applications, using my best handwriting, and I answered every question, even the ones for which I had no answers. And in the dreams and in life I was told, No work now. Try again in a month. I'll put your application on file.

21

My first job was at the food counter in a variety store downtown. I was hired as a temp, filling in for a woman on family leave. I microwaved sandwiches, kept the coffeepot filled, and served juice, soda, whatever the customer ordered. "Easy deal," Pamela said. I was sure she was right, but every day I seemed to find something else to do wrong. I served coffee that was too hot or not hot enough, didn't smile enough for some people ("You ever crack that little poker face of yours?") and didn't talk enough for others ("Cat got your tongue, honey?"). I gave people too little change or too much. The man I'd shorted glared, as if I meant to steal his quarter. The woman I handed a ten instead of a one handed it back. Lucky for me. Some nights, I hardly slept for thinking about all this. Even though I was surrounded by food, I kept losing weight.

When Mindy, the woman I was filling in for, came back, she inspected the counter and the machines and the refrigerator. "Clean," she approved. Then she looked me over. "Sweetie, are you one of those anorexic types?" she asked. She made me a hamburger and stood over me while I ate it. I liked her freckled face, and I was happy when she said she was going to ask the boss to keep me on as her helper. At first he said no. Then he came back and said okay, but only until the end of the summer.

By then we had moved into an apartment, which Mr. Elias had helped us find. Bradley Towers sounded grand, but it was just three tall concrete boxes set around a big parking lot with some grass and trees. I was fifteen now. I had my Social Security number, and lying about my age no longer made my stomach ache. Every day I went to work. Sometimes Pamela did things in the apartment, made a meal or mopped the floor, but mostly she just fed herself and watched TV. Toward the end of the year, she started a project to make a quilt with scraps. She got tired of it, though, and instead made her first Monica, a knitted doll.

She talked about it as if it were alive. She perched her on the back of the couch and warned me not to pick her up. "She doesn't like anyone but me to touch her." She said that the Monica — and, later on, the first Mortie — was there to watch me.

"She sees everything you do." The Monica's eyes were flat black buttons, and they did seem to follow me around the room, to be gazing fixedly at me, no matter where I was. After a while, they were the first things my eyes went to when I came home every day.

After the counter job, I had a whole series of jobs. I handed out flyers for a store opening, baby-sat in a sports club, washed windows in a florist shop, and sold pretzels in a closet-sized booth in a mall. Some of my jobs lasted a week, some as long as three or four months. Every job ended for a different reason. I worked in a knitting store until the owner, a tall wide-hipped woman, asked if I could lend her money. When I said I didn't have any, she nodded in an unsurprised way and said there wasn't enough business to keep me on anyway, and I might as well pick up my check and not return.

Sometimes when I lost a job, Pamela threw food on the floor or knocked over books and lamps. Once she swept all the glasses out of the cupboard. It took me hours, crawling around on the floor, to find every tiny shard. She sat on the couch, Mortie and her first and second Monica behind her, all of them watching me.

I lost the pretzel-shop job because of a pimple on my chin. Pamela didn't believe me. "Did the boss say that?"

"No."

"What'd he say?"

"Said he didn't need me anymore. He was cutting back."

"So why'd you lie to me?"

"I didn't. It's the pimple." I had seen him staring at it. I had seen the expression on his face.

"Don't give me that crap. What'd you do, steal?" She heaved herself out of her chair, her cheeks puffy and streaked raw. I backed away, but she came after me. In this mood, she could move fast. She bumped me into the wall, pulled me, and knocked me to the floor. She kicked me. When she was through, she cried. She always cried afterward. One time, she punched her hand into the wall and said it was my fault it happened; I'd made her do it, and she never would have, if it wasn't for me and my big mouth.

I thought she might be right. I told myself to be more careful, not to blurt everything out. Why tell her I had lost this job or that? Why say anything I didn't have to? But when I walked into the apartment and saw the Morties and the Monicas staring at me, I felt they knew everything anyway.

It was spring again. My birthday was close, my third without Mother. One morning, very early, I left the apartment. I had lost another job a few days before. My face was still bruised and tender, but heading into the cool air I was jubilant, as if I'd carried off an amazing feat. Maybe I had. I'd gotten out of the apartment without waking Pamela. I walked the streets for a long time. The sun rose. Slowly, my jubilation wore off. There was nowhere to go. I put on sunglasses to cover my swollen eyes. I was tired and I felt old.

In a diner, I ordered coffee and sat in a booth, listening to people talking and joking. Their voices slapped over me like a big wash of water. They were blurs, big loose shapes sitting on the stools, moving and swaying, like beasts with voices, the words indistinguishable. I wondered if I was going crazy.

I got up and left. In a park I almost fell down on a bench. I thought of Pamela sitting in her chair, waiting for me to return. She would sit there and wait, and wait, and wait. What if I never went back? What if I started walking and didn't stop until I was far away? What would happen to Pamela? Who would shop for her, who would cook, set traps for the roaches, and bring her mystery books from the library? Who would watch out for her and be good to her? Who would be the good girl?

I got a job in a gift shop. The store was owned by Hallie Langstrom. She was tall and pretty, with curly gray hair. She'd had three husbands and four children, she told me, and had traveled all over the world. She took an interest in me and said I should pin my hair up in a French knot and never wear yellow. She gave me other advice, and I listened to everything she said, and sometimes told her things too. But not about Pamela. Not why I had bruises. It was like being in eighth grade and wanting to write only pretty words for Mrs. Karyl.

Hallie was like Mrs. Karyl in another way too, saying I could do things I'd never done. "You should be in college," she said one day, when she saw me reading on lunch break. "You're intelligent. I want you to have a plan." She looked at me as if she really cared if I had that plan. "Save your money and go to school, Em."

"All right," I said, as if I could do that. As if it were a real thing.

I started waiting for poems again, then, for words. I had never really stopped, just put it off. I thought

I might tell Hallie about Mrs. Karyl but before I could she told me she was closing down the shop. "I'm declaring bankruptcy. I've been losing money for months. I'm going the Chapter Seven route."

"What?"

"This is my last day open to the public. I won't need you after today. I can inventory and pack up, all that, myself."

"What about me?" I said.

"What about you?"

"This is my job."

"Oh, you'll get another one. You'll be all right," she said, as if she hardly knew me, as if we'd never talked about anything. "You're young," she added.

After he hired me to be his assistant, Mr. Pumero could never seem to remember my name. He started with the *E* and then couldn't stop. He called me Emily or Emeline or Evelyn or even Ermingrave. "Em is just too short for him, I guess," I said to Pamela. I made her laugh, reciting the names he called me.

Every day I brought her little cakes, cookies, candy bars or doughnuts, and stories about Mr. Pumero and his customers. I made the people who came into his hardware store silly types who stumbled around, fumbling with money and credit cards, falling in the aisles, sending boxes and pails crashing to the floor.

"Heh-heh-heh-heh," Pamela would laugh, hitting herself on the head. "You're killing me." The crazier I made it, the more destruction there was, the more she liked it. The nights she laughed were the good nights. The nights that weren't so good were when she chewed hard on her food and nothing I said was funny. There was no way to know how those nights would end. No way to know if, in the morning, I would move slowly and carefully, and cover myself with long sleeves, makeup, and sunglasses.

"What's the matter with you, Emeline, wearing dark glasses?" Mr. Pumero said. He had a square, close-cropped head. "There's no sun in here."

I tried for a smile, tried to walk as quickly as usual, to work as hard as ever. My back hurt and my eyes were wet behind the concealing lenses. When the phone rang, I knew it was Pamela, even before I picked up. "Pumero's," I said. "How may I help you?"

"Em! Is that you, Em? What are you doing?"

"I'm working, Pamela." I kept the phone close to my lips. She had fallen into the habit of calling me. "Is there something you have to tell me, Pamela?"

"Hey! Can't I say hello if I want to say hello? You

got something against me saying hello? I just want to say hello to my little sis, so I say hello." It was her way of apologizing.

I glanced over at Mr. Pumero at his desk. He was watching me. "You really shouldn't call me here," I said quietly.

"Hey!" she shouted. "Hey! Hey! Don't talk to me like that. It's a free country, in case you forgot! I'll pick up the damn phone and talk to you any damn time I want to."

I knew she liked the sound of all that. I heard the rough sparkle in her voice.

"Was that your sister again?" Mr. Pumero said one day, after Pamela had called for the second time.

"Yes, sir."

"This is a business, Emily. She shouldn't be calling here."

"I know. I'm sorry."

"Well, don't be sorry. Just tell her to cut out the calls. I don't mind once in a while, but this is a business," he repeated.

"I'll tell her," I said.

After supper that night, I tried to talk to her about it. She barely let me get through my first sentence. "And just who the hell does he think he is?"

"He's the boss, Pamela."

"And that means he can tell me what to do? He can't tell me what to do. Can he tell me what to do, Monica?" She turned to the doll, her hands on her hips. "No, he can't!" she said in the Monica voice.

"It's his business, Pamela. He owns it. He's the boss." I said all the things I'd said before. "He doesn't want the phone tied up. A customer might be trying to call."

"Well, screw him and his business and his customers, and his crazy nutty frucking memory. I'll call you when I want to, and you can tell him I said so."

22

A few days after Mr. Pumero fired me, I told Pamela I was going out to buy a loaf of bread. "I'll be right back," I said. I put on sunglasses to cover my eyes and a jacket to cover my arms. In my pocketbook, I had stuffed a pair of underpants and a blouse. I wanted to take Mother's green sweater, the one with the cat buttons, but I couldn't find it. I hadn't seen it for a long time. Pamela said I must have misplaced it.

I walked downtown to the bus station and bought a ticket to Burlington, Vermont. I chose Burlington abstractly: it could have been anywhere, as long as it was somewhere else. And I chose it specifically, because in one of the places where I'd worked — the print shop, I think — I'd heard someone speak about Vermont as if it were a place apart. Another world: beautiful, green, special. "Oh, Vermont," he'd said, and his voice was full of awe. "Vermont is magic!" I thought it must be a place where people had to do nothing to be happy, only live there.

On the bus, traveling north on Route 22A, I sat on the left side of the aisle and stared in a daze at Lake Champlain and the mountains beyond. I touched the lump over my eye and wondered what I would do in Burlington. I had no plans, beyond finding some place to sleep. That turned out to be the Y. I went to bed and slept for ten hours. In the morning, I walked around the city, looking at the old houses with their big lawns. I bought bread in a market and sat by the lake, eating it with cheese and an apple. Before I went to sleep, I washed my clothes and hung them to dry at the foot of the bed.

The next day I did all the same things: walked down to the water and then up the hills to the college. I ate bread and oranges. I was calm. I seemed to float in Vermont's blue air. I had the sensation that there were two of me: moving together, yet separate, one hovering over the other.

For a week I lived this way, thinking no farther than the next corner I would turn, the next street I would walk down, the next apple I would eat. There were still piles of snow melting at the corners, the sun was pale yellow, the sky blue as a crayon.

One night, I called Pamela from an outdoor phone booth. "How are you doing on your own?" I had rehearsed saying this.

"Em? Where the hell are you?"

"Vermont."

"Ver-mont?" she said. "Ver-mont. I figured you for dead."

"Not yet," I said.

"This dump is quiet without you. I suppose you want me to say I miss you? I don't miss you one stinking bit, how about that? You like that? You left me, you little bitch, I had no food, I went shopping and all these stinking people wouldn't leave me alone, they were cheating me."

"What happened?" I asked.

"A lot of noise. Forget it. You coming back or not?"

Not, I thought. And then, *Say it.* My stomach lurched. "You hit me again."

"What?"

"You hit me."

"So?"

"I don't want you to do that."

"It's not my damn fault. What am I supposed to do, you come home and say sorrr-y! Sorrry I lost the job. Sorry! And now you say it's my fault? You got me going — you know you shouldn't have done that, you know how I am, I can't help it. And then you walk out on me. What a sister. You think that's nice?"

In the street, a truck ground by. I took in breath and let it out and tried to think of nothing. To think only of walking the streets, the sky like a shelf over my head.

"Why don't you just come home?" she said.

I leaned against the wall, staring out the little window of the phone booth. "I don't want you to hit me," I said again.

Then — as if that were a reasonable request, and I should certainly have mentioned it sooner — she said, Okay-okay-fine and if I had to know, she missed me, she really had missed me.

When I walked into the apartment, she was sitting in her chair, her legs spread out. She looked at me. So did the Monicas and Morties.

"Hello, Pamela," I said.

She got up and came toward me. "So you came home," she said. She reached out for me and kissed me. Then she held me away from her and looked at me again. "Well, damn!" she said. She took my face between her hands and squeezed. "Well, damn!" she said again, and squeezed my cheeks so hard I thought the bones would crack. "You little turd," she said, squeezing harder and harder.

PART III

The Doubled Moon

23

The Morties and Monicas eye me from the back of the couch. That's their job. To watch me every minute of every day. Like Pamela, their creator. *Em Em, look at my darling new Mortie.* Sitting in her chair, long yellow needles clicking. *Look at his sticky wicky, his little micky: squeeze it, don't be shy.* Six Morties, six Monicas, leaning against each other, tongues sticking out, watching me with flat black eyes. I could strangle them, one by one. I want to. I want to kill them. I have wanted to kill them for a long time. My heart tightens with this desire.

The Morties' ties dangle, the Monicas' ponytails are like stiff brushes. Look at their eyes, look how they follow me around the room, how they glare. Pamela's little sentries. I sweep my hand across the top of the couch, knock them this way and that, pitch them into each other. I make another sweep and topple them to the floor, where they lie in a heap.

And now Pamela's chair is glowering. The tattered arms are huge, menacing. "Say nothing," I warn and shove it into a corner, fast, the way I threw down the Morties and Monicas. For a moment I feel brilliant, daring. I jump on the spot where the chair has always been, the place from which it could not be moved, not an inch, not a fraction of an inch — and if it happened, the penalty was severe. My ear throbs with memory, the ear she grabbed and tore. I jump again and land with a hard smack of feet. *Crazy crazy loony nuts I always knew,* Pamela yells, and I jump again and again and only stop when the old man downstairs, Mr. Foster, smacks the ceiling — BOOM-BOOM-BOOM — with his broom.

24

After Mother died, the thought came to me (and I couldn't imagine then that it wasn't thought, but mute, passionate longing stuck to the chaos of feeling like dust to glue) that if I was good, if I paid attention, if I put up with, if I understood and overlooked and (later on) tended my bruises in silence, I believed – I can see now I needed to believe – that, in time, happiness would be given me. That I would find it. Or it would find me.

It was this belief, like a small, steady breath in my

heart, that kept alive Mother's old command to me —
Be good, Em — kept it alive long after I should have forgotten it. I mean, why? Why did I go on believing?
Did it make sense? Why did I go on thinking, even
when Pamela slammed me around, that if you are
good enough, patient enough, for long enough, your
reward will come?

25

"I heard about your sister," Mrs. Shotwell cries, swinging down the hall toward me on her crutch. "I've been trying to remember her name. Phyllis, was it?"

"Pamela," I say, holding open the door to the trash room.

"Is that so?" she says disbelievingly.

We're both holding our garbage, hers such a neatly wrapped and tied package that it makes me ashamed of my old garbage. Mine doesn't look nearly as good, just two lumpy paper bags. And from her glance, I'm afraid I'm not looking much better in my old jeans and torn sneakers.

"It was plaguing me all morning," she says. "Her name. I finally remembered. Phyllis."

"Pamela," I repeat.

She frowns as if I've got it wrong again. "I never saw her much. She kept to herself, didn't she? How old are you, dear?"

"Twenty-one," I say. The lie comes automatically.

Mrs. Shotwell clicks her tongue. "So young to be alone," she says, giving me a sad face. She wears her hair the same old-fashioned way Mother did, wound around her head in a single thick braid.

That hair was the reason I went to her apartment once in the middle of the night. The floor was quiet, the whole building was dead quiet. I knocked on her door for a long time. At last it opened a crack and she peered out. "What?" she said. "What is it?" I held out my bruised arms. She looked at them, then at me, then closed the door quietly, and again I heard the silence of the house. I stood there waiting, although for what I didn't know. When I went back to the apartment, my feet were enormously cold, like two lumps of dead flesh.

"At least it was quick for your sister," she says. "Now my poor husband, poor Jack." Her voice sing-songs. "Poor Jack, he lingered. Oh, he lingered – I had such a time with him. I didn't sleep for weeks."

I could tell her that I haven't been sleeping well, either. I could say that the apartment is too quiet, that Pamela's ranting voice — *Why don't you do something sitting there like a lump never going to move you'll be as dead as me* — is the only thing that breaks apart the silence.

This morning, though, I did it. I broke the silence. I took a hammer to the lock on Pamela's cupboard, smashing it open. I was eager to see what was inside. Money, I hoped, thinking of the way she had hidden Father's money under the trailer. What I found, though, were all the things I'd "lost" through the years. A pair of garnet earrings that had been Mother's, a china dog that Lois had given me, a bracelet I'd made out of yarn one summer, and Mother's green sweater, the one that I'd "misplaced." It was full of holes; moths had got into it. There were other things as well. Rags, crumpled balls of aluminum foil, toothless combs, pencil stubs, stained underpants, tubes of dried medicine.

"Your sister —" Mrs. Shotwell hesitates, like someone stepping on a wet floor and trying not to leave footprints. "She was an, ah, interesting person."

I shift the soggy trash bags. "You mean crazy," I say. "A liar, a hitter, a crazy person."

No. I don't say it. The words press against my throat like solid objects, but rise no further.

"Mr. Bielic says it was a stroke." Mrs. Shotwell makes a prim mouth. "He told me when he came up to fix my showerhead. So young to have a stroke!" She makes that mouth again, as if Pamela's dying is proof of some disgusting secret.

Suddenly, perversely, I wish for Pamela. For my sister. Who else can I tell about Mrs. Shotwell's disapproving little mouth? Who else can I amuse with my stories? Who else is going to shout in her most affectionate tone when I make her laugh, "Oh, you bad, bad little girl!"

Mrs. Shotwell drops her garbage into one of the silver cans and sighs. "You think someone is going to be with you forever, and then they're gone. Life is mysterious."

I grip my two bags of garbage in both arms, as if they're something to hang on to forever. "Death, even more so," I blurt.

One day you are alive: you blow your nose, you take a walk, you eat, you sleep, and day passes day, and maybe you're a good person and maybe you're not, but it doesn't matter, because after a while, good or bad, there comes another day, and you are dead. Mother died. Pamela died. I will die. Everyone dies. Everyone, without exception, lives and then dies. A stubborn, unrelenting pattern; commonplace, mysterious.

I will never truly understand — not why we have to

die, or how it happens from one second to another. How Mother was alive and then she was dead. How Pamela lay on the rug, her furious eye fastened on me. And time passed, and I thought she might lie there forever, never letting me go. Then in the blink of a second, the light of her eye was gone. She was gone.

It happened. It had to happen. But of course, it is not as clear as all that, either. There is the phone call I could have made sooner, and the "time factor." Isn't that what they always say in mystery shows, the time factor?

Something is dripping on the floor, a tiny rain of liquid. Just as I notice this, Pamela shrieks in my ear *Serves you right smelly prying bitch* and at the same moment the garbage bags stretch and sigh, and then, like Pamela's revenge, they both give way. Coffee grounds, eggshells, the Morties and Monicas, and all the foul-smelling rags from Pamela's cupboard spill on me and the floor and spatter Mrs. Shotwell's gleaming, laced-up shoes.

She stamps her foot. "Get that cleaned up," she orders, as if it's her own pristine floor that's been debased, and hobbles to the door.

She didn't have to say it. I'm already down on my knees.

26

In the middle of the night, Pamela's litany yanks me out of my sleep. *What happened where were you you're late what did you do where's the money I'm hungry make supper get a move on do you have something to tell me I'm dying for a laugh when the hell are you going to do the laundry wash the dishes give me a haircut clean this place you don't know how good you have it —*

Her voice is in my head, in the air, in the room. I fall out of bed and run through the apartment: but her voice follows me, a jackhammer blasting my brain with words. When it finally stops, I creep back into bed and lie there, my heart shaking my whole body. Suddenly I leap out again, cross the space between our beds and run my hand over the covers, feeling for her heat in the mattress – and even when nothing moves under my touch, looking to make sure she's not there, humped in a corner, big bulging eyes open and watching me.

The only time I escaped those eyes was at night. She slept hard and deep, as if sleep were a passion. Solid, dead-and-gone sleep, that was her sleep. Baby sleep. The sleep of the innocent, she told me once: nothing on *my* conscience, she said. And she hit herself on the head, overcome with laughter, because I never slept that way.

27

A dream: I'm standing in front of a long narrow mirror. Someone is telling a story, maybe the one about Snow White. There seems to be a glass coffin here. I search the room. "I've mislaid a sister," I say. Pamela is behind me. She's coming for me. Breath pumps in my throat, my heart runs me into the ground, propels me like a fist as hard as iron. I'm not fat and strong like her. No, don't! I shout, but it's done. I'm darkness, I'm dead.

*   *   *

Another dream: Pamela's big hand. A hand like meat. No, I say, no. But she's laughing at a joke I made, so I know it's going to be okay this time. I wake up dazed.

A third dream: Rotting bodies of giant mice heaped in a room. The smell is disgusting. I want to get out of this room! The door is far away, but in the distance, I see flowers like heaps of gold across the top of a train, and someone is saying that I should get on board. *Hurry — hurry up, you'll miss it!*

From the last dream, I wake up knowing that there's something I need to do, though I can't think what it is. Later, in the market, the first thing I see is a revolving rack of flower seed packets. Marigold, lemon balm, calendula. The same flowers that Mother planted all around her vegetable garden. Alyssum, sweet william, lupine. I look at the pictures on the packets and say each beautiful beautiful name to myself.

28

I'm waiting for the elevator when a woman comes in through the front door. Nothing exceptional about that: people go in and out that door all day, every day. Old men shuffling their feet; boys who've parked motorcycles outside, and mothers with kids hanging off them like clothespins.

I see tinted glasses, a green shirt, a hand pulling a scarf off dark hair.

The shirt's the same green as Mother's cat-button sweater. That's what I notice first. Then her face:

cheekbones, little lines around her mouth, an I-don't-see-you gaze. And her hair — dark, thick, almost wild.

I stare at her in the first moment as if I know her better than anyone in the world, although I've never seen her before. In the second moment, I know this is wrong: I have seen her and in exactly this way — me waiting for the elevator with my handful of junk mail, she making a high-shouldered beeline for the stairs. I can't understand how I could have forgotten her even for an instant. But in the reign of Pamela, I lived as in another dimension of time, the world passing in a blur before my eyes. Who I saw, I barely saw. What I felt, I hardly grasped.

Lobby, elevator, mailboxes, door, stairs, door. This has been my round for the past half hour. I'm looking for the woman with the dark hair and green shirt. Walk through the lobby, look out the front door, check the elevator, check the mailboxes, go to the stairwell, start all over again.

William gazes at me with his mouth open.

"You're drooling," I say.

"What?" He's sitting on the bench against the wall.

I take a tissue from my pocket, wipe his mouth.

"Thanks, Em!" He giggles and cranes his neck.

I want to talk to her. I don't know how I'll do it, what I'll say. Start with hello, I guess.

Hello. Hello, my name is Em. Hello. What's your name?

Baby talk. William talk. Don't I know how to do it any other way? I think so, but I'm out of practice. If I could only grab her mind and pull it into mine, then she'd see who I am and how she's been walking around in there for days, shoving everything else aside.

Outside, little girls are playing jump rope; there's a knot of guys bent over the open hood of a car. I cross the parking lot, walk to the sidewalk, look both ways.

In again. Lobby, elevator, mailboxes, door.

Hello, please don't think I'm rude. Hello. I just want to know your name. Hello, I'm Em. Maybe we can be friends. Please.

No, not please. Not humble. Her face wouldn't like that.

Maybe she'll be the one to start. Hello there! I noticed you by the elevator the other day. Aren't you the girl with the sister who died? And now you're all alone. . . .

She'll link arms with me, we'll go somewhere, a coffee shop. I'll tell her that once I worked in a place like this. But not for too long. I fumbled a pitcher of juice, spilled it all over a customer. She'll laugh. I'll tell her about the different places I worked. Just funny stories to make her laugh again.

Another time, maybe the next time, I could tell her about Vermont, and some things about Pamela. How I hardly worked after I came back. My sister's disability checks provided for us, I'll say. It wasn't much, but after Vermont she hated to have me go out. She didn't want me to be away from her. She was suspicious even when I went to the library for her. At the end, she wouldn't let me out even for food; we called in our grocery orders. I didn't leave the apartment for weeks, months.

No. I can't say all that. If I say it, she'll think I'm crazy. Anyway, you can't tell everything at once. I used to do it. Tell too much, too fast. I'll be careful. I won't blurt. I won't embarrass. I'll ask her about herself. Where do you work? I'll say. Do you like your job? I want to know everything about you. Do you like flowers?

29

"We got nice trees and grass here, what do you want flowers for?" Mr. Bielic tips back in his chair and looks up at the pipes crossing the ceiling.

"Flowers are pretty. They're nice for everybody," I say, trying to look appealing.

"You got it pretty here already, plus no work." He twists a lock of graying hair. "All you got to do is go outside, sit on a bench under a tree, sniff the air. The grass is mowed, everything is nice, you don't have to do nothing."

"A garden is different. It could just be marigolds."
Mother always had a garden. In the fall she gave the
extra stuff away by the bagful: squash, onions, turnips,
all kinds of things. Once, someone gave her an apple
pie in return — it was delicious.

"A garden is work. Take my word for it. I have
enough work already."

"Not you. Me. I'll do it. I'll do everything. Just a
little garden, I won't ask you for anything."

"Yeah, that's what they all say." He sounds gloomy.
"There's rules here. The problem's not me."

"Marigolds, that's all — a few marigolds. I won't
ask you for anything." *Saying the same thing again retard
can't you try another line of bull at least.* Pamela's voice
comes through like someone on a fuzzy phone line. I
hold out the packet of seeds, as if that will convince
him. "It would only be a small garden, not just for me.
For everyone." *Liar you won't let anyone get near it.* I turn
my face away from her voice. "I'll keep it neat, promise."

Mr. Bielic scratches his chest. The sound is like
the mice I hear in the walls at night. "If I do it for you,
I have to do it for everyone. People today want every-
thing. I was brought up different. Do things for myself.
Independence Day. Don't worry about Mr. Somebody
Else."

I nod. Isn't that what I want to do, something for
myself?

"If it was up to me, what do I care? You could have it. But the big problem is the Big Cheese. Understand? I'm not the Big C here, I'm just maintenance. What's he going to say? 'Bielic, you got enough to do keeping the halls and elevators clean, what do you want the grass messed up with a garden for!' And another thing, there's rules here."

He takes a piece of paper and reads out loud. "'No tenant should disturb the landscaping around the project or take it upon him or herself to cut, trim, or otherwise rearrange any of the foliage, leaves, et cetera, of the landscaping.'"

A familiar feeling overtakes me: a heaviness in the legs, a thickness like dust in my head. It won't happen. Nothing will change. I can't have what I want. I groveled in front of this man for nothing. I'm so stupid. Just what Pamela always said.

30

"No money! Where is it, where's the money? Where are you? I need you!" I'm pulling out drawers, knocking things to the floor. Talking to myself, to the walls, to the pocketbook I can't find. I race through the apartment, searching under the bed and behind the couch. What do I do now? I've lost my pocketbook. All my money's in it. Now what?

I'm sweating and breathing hard. *No money no money no money.* Pamela's with me today, she's been here from the moment I woke up, mocking and knocking in my ear. *Stupid got no money no money no money.* She won't stop, she loves to see me like this, crazy and out of control.

I find the pocketbook in the bathroom and sit on the tub and count the bills and change. Count once, then twice. Then once more to be sure there's really so little left. I sit on the edge of the tub, and I don't listen to Pamela. I won't. I can't. I concentrate, because I have to remember all the things you're supposed to do when you look for work.

You get dressed up and you go around to different places, and you fill out applications and say you have experience selling and you're ready to do anything. And then they tell you they don't want you, they don't need you, and maybe you can come back and try again in a month or six months. And you feel bad, because people keep telling you they don't want you, but even so, you have to do it again the next day. Just do it and pretend it's okay, pretend you don't mind how awful you feel when they look you up and down, or don't look at you at all, or laugh a little and say, "Sorry, no work."

I scrub my fingernails, shower, wash my hair. I go through all my clothes to find something that's not torn, stained, old. I put on a dress I'd forgotten I had, blue and white, with white buttons down the front. I polish my shoes and do my fingernails again, and look at my face in the mirror. No pimples anyway. I change my dress for a skirt and blouse, then change back to the dress again. I brush my hair. How do I look? Will someone want me? I go out the door, then come back in and rinse my mouth to make sure my breath is okay.

Half the day has gone by then, but I go downtown and walk around, and go in my first store and ask if they need someone to work.

No.

I go in another store. No.

No. No. No.

31

Walking across the parking lot, I see the dark-haired woman again. She's getting out of a faded blue car. She locks the doors. Then we're walking directly toward each other. I lift a hand, start a smile. Her eyes pass over me as if I'm nothing. Nothing to her. Nothing to anyone. We pass each other without speaking.

On the radio someone is singing: "Baby baby baby, I sure could use some good new-eews today." Tears spurt out of my eyes. I've been crying for days. I never cried before. All these years I never cried. I was proud of it. Brave little me. Now I'm crying and I can't stop. Crying and sleeping. Nothing but dreams and tears. First I sleep, then I cry, then I walk around in a wet-faced daze. And if I fall asleep again, I dream about tears, a field of red tears.

Pamela returns. She enters through several walls, climbs in the window, waits for me in the bathtub. It's daylight, so I know I'm not dreaming. She shakes the apartment with her rage.

My body vibrates: my bones clatter like teeth.

You screwed yourself, she says. *Look at you, you're a mess. You need me,* she screams, in her deep crazy passionate voice.

32

Exactly like the first time, I'm waiting for the elevator when the front door opens, and the dark-haired woman comes in and heads for the stairwell. I want to speak, and I can't. Everything I've thought of to say to her drains out of my mind. I stare at the signs on the walls:

NO LITTERING
NO LOUD NOISES
NO SMOKING
NO SPITTING

NO RUNNING

NO BARE FEET

I read each sign as if I've never seen it before. My neck is as rigid as a post. My back is frozen. My legs will never move again. Only my ears, like two animals that have nothing to do with me, are alert, springing out from my head, listening for her steps.

"The elevator's coming," someone says in a loud, terrible voice. A voice like Pamela's voice. Like a moose bellowing. A train heading for a crash.

"The elevator's coming!" the voice brays.

"Excuse me?" She turns. "Are you talking to me?"

I point to the arrow creeping toward the first floor. "It's coming." I whisper this time.

She will think I am crazy. Pamela agrees in my ear, cackling away. *Crazy loony mad crazy crazy loony* —

"Stairs are better for your health," she says. "Probably faster than that slow boat to China too."

Slow boat? I think. China? And then she's gone, through the door, out of sight.

I get in the elevator. The door closes, the elevator doesn't move. That's okay. I'll just stand here and think about her. How I spoke to her, how she answered. I rearrange the conversation in my head. Make it slower, more leisurely. I say hello in a quiet voice. She responds with a smile. I say, Excuse me, the elevator's coming. She says, Oh, thank you, but I like taking the stairs —

Suddenly I understand two things: *I* made the real conversation happen. And the elevator's not moving because I haven't pushed the button.

On the fifth floor, the overhead lights are flickering again and the hall is dim. No matter. I could walk here blindfolded and find my way. I know every bump in the floor, every crack in the wall. Tan walls, brown doors, black floor. Smells of meat cooking, sounds of babies, TVs, and dogs. I must have smelled these smells and heard these sounds a thousand times. Then why is this like the first time? Have I been asleep all these years? Am I awake now — alive at last?

33

Once, in grade school, our class was taken on an overnight excursion to a campground. The air was warm: we had a campfire and ate hot dogs; and as darkness fell, we were herded down to the lake. There were perhaps thirty children, so I suppose there were at least four or five adults. We trooped through the woods with flashlights. There must have been yelling and singing, the grown-ups chattering. A noisy expedition. At the shore of the lake we were presented, as if on a stage, with a doubled moon — one floating in the clear dark sky, one in the clear dark calm of the water.

Were there exclamations, shouts of amazement, loud giggly praise for this sight? There might have been, but for me there was only silence. An unprecedented silence, tranquil and immense. Silence, and the moon on the lake — a sight so pure I nearly staggered under its impact. I knew, without the words to say it, that the lack in my life of what this moon and lake represented was the other side of the coin of happiness. Not unhappiness, but shame, which was possibly the same thing, and which then rose up in me in nauseating waves. Shame for my disorderly, precarious home. Shame because we were different from everyone I knew. Shame because we lived in a trailer, because my father drank too much and my mother was sick, shame because my sister was crazy, and I was small and scared.

I wondered how I had lived without knowing such calm was possible, that such pure peace existed. Without being able to phrase any of this in these words and terms, I remember quite clearly wanting this for myself, feeling almost dizzy with the force of the wanting.

Standing in that doubled light, I felt that I had

stumbled on a truth, which was simply this: if I had
it — "it" being not the moon and the lake, as such, not
its stark and startling beauty, but the *itness* of it — if
I had that, I could finally be happy and like other
people.

34

The dark-haired woman is sorting through envelopes in the mail alcove as I walk in. "Junk, junk, junk," she says, and drops a handful of envelopes into the wastebasket. I fumble with my mailbox key, glance quickly at her.

When she leaves, I reach into the basket for one of the discarded envelopes. Louise D'Angelo is her name. She lives in 7M.

* * *

Norma Fox Mazer

The seventh floor is different from my floor: there are more doormats laid out, the ceiling light is better. Apartment 7M is at the far end of the hall. A sign is taped below the knocker: THANK YOU FOR NOT SMOKING. A smiley-face makes the period. I touch the smiley-face with the tips of my fingers.

Someone is telling a story in a shadowy room. I pay no attention, just go on searching in every corner for someone. I know who I'm looking for, I just can't remember the name right now. This is probably a dream, I think, but maybe not. I want her to see the sky. It's amazing. Enormous stars all over the place, every one a different color. She strolls toward me. "Louise!" I cry out. There are so many things I have to tell her. How I long for transformation. How much I want to be like her: defined, strong.

Walking across the field behind the building, I'm saying her name under my breath. Louise D'Angelo. Louise the Angel. A perfect, perfect name. I'm happy thinking about her until money and jobs sneak into my mind. Rain spatters the ground. A wind springs up and drives bits of paper into the bushes. Mother used to say, "You'll never go hungry with a garden." I could

165

make a garden right here where I'm walking. It's just a big empty field, full of nothing but trash and weeds. Nobody cares about it. One little garden wouldn't even be noticed.

I drag a stick in the ground, marking off a rectangle behind some bushes. Stones poke out of the ground everywhere, and the soil is as dry as dust. I could bury my food garbage here, plant over it. Mother always had a pail of potato peels and fish bones for her garden. I could plant chives, chard, lettuce: garlic too, but not until Columbus Day. And marigolds, little gold heads to smell good and keep away the bugs. *Frucking crazy nuthead,* Pamela bawls. My arms fly up to push her away. The wind and rain come down hard and I take off, running. I haven't run like this in years. I get into a rhythm, pump my arms, and run straight across the field.

35

"Hello, Em!" William sits down next to me on the bench.

"Hello, William."

"You can sit here."

"Thank you, William." There's spit on his chin.

"Are you happy today, Em?"

If I see Louise D'Angelo, I'll be happy.

I have things to tell her. That I've started using the stairs. That I've been up and down them a dozen times already. They're empty, so empty. My steps drum, the gray cement walls echo, I hold my breath from landing to landing.

"You look happy today," William says. "Are you really, really happy?" His voice rises, sings out *really, really.* "You're pretty, Em."

"Thank you, William. You always say that."

He giggles. "Want to go for a walk?"

"Not now." I hand him a tissue. "Dry your chin."

"What?"

"Your chin. Dry it."

"What? I can't hear you." He puts his hand to his ear.

"Your chin, William. There's stuff on it."

"What? What? I can't hear you." He laughs and slaps his knee. "Fooled you, didn't I? I fool my mommy a lot. Fooled you, Em, fooled you good."

If I see her, I'll nod, say hello. That's all. Reserved. Dignified. No yelling. She'll say hello too, maybe smile. I'll walk toward the stairwell. We'll go up together.

"What?" William says.

"I didn't say anything."

"You didn't say anything?"

"No."

"Yes you did. You said 'No'! Ha-ha-ha," he sings. "I got a tease on you!"

I'll be casual. I'll say, I always use the stairs now. Since you recommended it.

The front door swings opens, and Mr. Hunniger comes in. He's ninety-four and tiny, with a face like a creased paper bag.

"Hello, Mr. Hunniger!" William sings.

"William, my boy." Mr. Hunniger walks with fast little shuffling steps. "Did you make yourself rich today?"

William rocks on the bench, cackling. " 'Did you make yourself rich today!' 'Did you make yourself rich today?' That's good, Mr. Hunniger, that's a good joke!"

I'll tell her I use the elevator now only when I have packages.

She'll say: So, the fifth floor is where you live.

Yes, I'll say. What's your floor?

We'll walk up together. We'll talk. I'll tell her about writing down words again and keeping them. Maybe I wrote a poem. Probably not, probably it's just a bunch of words that I got in my head. She'll say: Can I see this? Can I read it?

Pamela shouted in my ear the whole time I was writing the words. I knew she'd hate them. I wrote as fast as I could. *Kicking up heels breath a bellow tongue hanging out like a dog. Jackass dog monkey, you menagerie, you human zoo. Darling, did she do it, make you the dog the jackass in harness leather tight around the heart oh darling oh little girl your tears your tears.* Pamela kept shouting, like spitting into my brain. I threw away the paper to stop her, to shut her up. I cried. I didn't cry when Mother died, and now I'm crying all the time, crying about nothing, about a piece of paper, a handful of words.

In the middle of the night I got up and fished the paper out of the trash. Even though I didn't really need it: I knew the words by heart. I memorized them. I always memorize things, ever since she tore up my notebook. Because even if you can't write, you can say words in your mind, and if you keep saying them to yourself, after a while they're like a little tower of blocks that can't be toppled. They're there in your mind. You remember them. For a long time, I did that. Then I stopped. That was after Vermont. I couldn't get away from her then and I felt too bad. When she squeezed my face, it was as if she squeezed all the words out of me.

"You're pretty, Em," William says. There's spit on his chin still. "I like girls. Did I tell you you're pretty?"

"Yes, William. Three times. Thank you, thank you, thank you."

He giggles. "That's three times too. Want to go for a walk?"

"I would rather sit here right now, William."

Two women with shopping bags and curled white hair come in from outside. "Hello, William," they say together. "How are you today, dear?" they say with one voice.

"I'm good today. This is my friend Em. She came to visit me and sit with me. Pretty soon, we're going to take a walk."

They smile at me. "Hello, Em," they say, with the same voice and the same smile they had for William. "How are you today, dear?" They give me kind smiles and bustle to the elevator.

I sit there, stupefied. Me and William? *Yeah you you you, you and your stupid words you and William —* Pamela's voice bangs in my ear; my heart bangs in my chest.

"Em," William says, "put your head up, Em. Put your head up. Are you laughing? What's funny? Tell me!"

"Nothing," I say, my voice muffled. "Nothing. Everything."

"One or the other," he cries. "Must choose, Em! Give me the right answer, Em. Nothing or everything?"

I look at his jolly, drooly face. "I don't know the answer."

"Oh, too bad!" He's sympathetic. "Are you getting sad? I get sad." He pinches his chin. "I'm retarded, you know."

"I know, William."

"Uh-huh! But you know what, I'll give you the answer to the question. Everything is the answer. That is the right answer. Everything is funny. I think so. Ha-ha-ha," he laughs to demonstrate. "Like, take life, Em. That's what my mommy says. Take life, she says, take life, it's very funny."

"Do you think so, William?"

He looks into my face. "Yes. Take life, it's very funny. So do you want to laugh? I do. I like to laugh." He shows me again. "Ha-ha-ha-ha," he cries mirthfully, and watches me for the effect.

36

"What're you doing?" the child says. She's wearing shorts and a dirty T-shirt. She stands over me, her hands on her flat little hips.

I don't answer. I'm on my hands and knees, punching at the ground with a trowel. Stone after stone turns up. I need a shovel for this work. Mother had a shovel, which she wouldn't let anyone else use. A good shovel is expensive, she said, but it's worth it. I don't dare carry a shovel in the building. If Mr. Bielic sees me, he's going to want to know why.

"What're you doing?" the child says again. She has straight hair and knees like little dirty doorknobs.

"What do you think I'm doing?" I pile the stones in a heap. I'll have a stone wall anyway, even if I don't have a garden.

"You playing a rock game?"

"No. Why don't you go away?"

"Want to know what you're doing."

"I'm trying to make a garden. Now, go away." Aren't children supposed to be cute? This one has a grim, downward cast to her face.

"Why you trying to make a garden?"

"Because I want to."

"What's that you're using?"

"A trowel."

"Why do you use a towel in a garden?"

"Not a towel, a trowel. Where'd you come from?"

"Over there."

"Over where?" More stones.

"Towers. Is that where you live too?"

"You better go back now." I stab at the ground. "Did you hear me? Go away, I'm busy."

"I ain't doing nothing. I don't have to go away." She squats down next to me. "Your towel is dirty. That's nasty."

"I told you, trowel. Trow. El."

"Trow. El."

"Right. It's like a little shovel."

"I know that," she says scornfully. "Why don't you have a big shovel?"

"Too much money."

She nods sympathetically. "I got a little shovel too. Want me to bring it?"

"No."

"Why not?"

"Nobody but me can do this."

"Why?"

"Why do you ask so many questions? Because it's mine."

"What's your name?"

"'Puddin' tame, ask me again and I'll tell you the same.'"

"My name's Lana and I'm this old." She holds up one hand, the fingers apart. "How old are you?"

"Old as the hills."

"How old are you really and truly?"

"Twenty-one."

"Whew!" She whistles between square baby teeth. "That's old. I got a sister that old."

I dig away at the soil, piling up rocks.

"When is your birthday?" she asks.

"April. When is yours?"

"August. August two-two. You know what that means? Twenty-two. August twenty-two is my true birthday. I'll be six. How old will you be on your true birthday?"

"I told you."

"Twenty-one?"

"Uh-huh."

"Is that your true true birthday age?"

I look at her. "What do you think?"

"I don't know. Is it your true true?"

"Sort of."

"Does that mean yes or no?"

"No. Can you keep a secret?"

She screws her face up tight. "I'm a good secret-keeper."

"Okay, then. I just turned eighteen."

She considers this, breathing heavily. "That's old, like twenty-one."

I don't know why I told her. It just fell out of my mouth. "You can't tell anybody," I say.

"Won't." She wraps her arms around her legs and settles herself more securely.

37

Someone's in the parking lot before me this morning. All week, I've carried my two plastic gallon-jugs of water out of the building without anyone seeing me. Every morning, I've watered the garden, weeded it, taken out more stones. This morning I overslept, and it's Louise out there in the parking lot, crossing toward the street. Seeing her, I forget everything — the garden and looking for work — and go after her.

I don't think about what I'm doing, I just do it. The sun is up, a hazy smear in the sky. She turns a corner and I do too. A bus passes, panting out pink exhaust fumes. She walks fast. I do too.

We climb a hill, cross another street. Trucks clog the road, gears grinding. She picks up the pace. "Brandon!" a girl yells out an opened window. The water bottles are getting heavy. I should dump them, but when I think of my sorry, dusty little garden, I can't bring myself to do it.

Stone angels with sleepy faces stare through a wire fence. We pass a diner, gas stations, a sound studio, a man sleeping in a doorway. Louise never looks back.

A crowd of women stops me. They're laughing and calling to one another, streaming through a factory gate. Suddenly I'm looking for Mother. I stand there and search for her, wait for her to walk by wearing her green sweater, intent on the day ahead of her. The women pass, one after the other, and when they're gone, swallowed by the factory, I still stand there, dazed. Maybe I'm dreaming. Dreaming the women, dreaming the water bottles hanging off the ends of my arms. Dreaming myself, scanning faces for Mother's face. Dreaming that I'm following Louise.

Louise! I don't see her anywhere. I rush on, past a shoe store, a cluster of little pink houses with tiny yards, a bakery with bread piled in the window, a computer store, another gas station. I'm at the corner before I realize that it was Louise I saw behind the counter in the bakery.

I turn back. At the bakery, I stand at the side of the window and look in. The walls are lined with shelves of bread. Round loaves and long loaves, baskets of rolls and bread sticks. Customers crowd the counter, and behind it are Louise in a white apron and a man wearing a sailor's cap. They're both wrapping bread, taking money, giving change.

The door opens, and a woman carrying an armful of long bread bags emerges. With her comes the smell of fresh bread and Louise's voice. The door bangs shut. I watch through the window for another moment, then walk back home. My arms ache from the weight of the water bottles. I like that ache. It's a real thing. It lets me know that I saw what I saw. I didn't dream it: Louise at work.

38

I stand outside her door. Just stand there and look at the smiley-face, and think about her. Then I sit down on the floor, in the corner, against the wall. I think how close she is. I think of her moving around her apartment, making a meal, sitting at the window to eat it. Suddenly the door opens, and it's her.

"What do you want?" she says. The look she gives me is awful.

I scramble to my feet, stammer hello.

"What are you doing here?" She folds her arms

across her chest. "You're following me, aren't you? I know you are."

"No, what do you mean?" My voice quivers.

"Look, do you think I'm stupid? I saw you. You followed me to work." She looks at my hands, as if she'll see the water bottles still hanging there.

"I'm sorry," I stammer. "I didn't mean, I didn't —"

"So it *was* you. I thought so. What is this anyway? Are you stalking me?"

"Oh, no, no, no."

"Just bad behavior?" she says. "Just really bad behavior?"

"I'm sorry. I just want to be friends."

"Oh, my God," she says, and steps back inside and shuts the door.

Lana's sprawled on her stomach, grubby hands playing around in the dirt. "What are you doing here?" I say. "Who said you could come here?"

"I'm waiting for the flowers." She twists her head to look up at me. "You said there'd be flowers. I don't see no flowers."

"They're sleeping. Go away."

"Where's their beds?" she says.

"Under the earth."

"Is that a fat lie?"

"No. That's the bed for seeds. Why don't you go away?"

"Do they like it in the bed? Is it nice and warm?"

"Yes." I get down on my knees and start weeding.

"What're you doing now? Want me to do that?"

"Don't touch!" I push away her hand. "You don't know what you're doing."

"I do too."

"No you don't. If you want to come here, you have to follow rules. And the rules are you don't do anything in this place unless I say so."

She gives me a weary shrug, as if she's heard this kind of stuff a thousand times before.

In the morning, it is always better — whatever *it* is. This is possibly the only rule of life I know for sure.

If, at night, I'm depressed and sad, then in the morning even if a shadow is still hanging over me, it'll be a smaller shadow. If the sadness is there, it's an edge of sadness: the border, not the whole dark blanket of it.

I guess I know one other rule of life. Take a walk, you'll feel better.

I do. I go for a walk. Try not to think about Louise. Try to believe something will change. Wait to feel better.

39

When Louise exits the stairwell door, I spring forward, holding up my index finger. "I've got a splinter, will you take it out for me?"

An odd smile lifts half her face, as if this is the most bizarre request she's ever heard. It probably is. I know people don't do things this way, just barge up to other people and start talking about splinters. But I meant to do it better, to say good morning first, to tell her that I was sorry about following her, and then ask about the splinter.

"All you need is a needle and peroxide," she says. She marches toward the front door.

I run alongside her. "No peroxide."

"Well, surely you have a needle?" She opens the door. A drizzle has turned the world gray. "Everyone has a needle," she says.

"I do," I say quickly. "I have a needle."

"There you go. Sterilize it with a match, and you're all set. Just poke away, and you'll get it out."

We're halfway across the parking lot. Suddenly she stops. "Are you following me again? What's going on? Who are you anyway?"

"I'm Em."

I say it, as if it explains everything. Why I followed her. Why I sat outside her door. How I got the splinter making a post for the garden and tried to get it out, but it was in too deep and I couldn't. How I woke up this morning thinking of her, of her name, Louise, Louise D'Angelo, thinking *Louise will take out the splinter.*

When I was alone, imagining it, it seemed so possible. She'd smile at me, say of course she'd help me, and we'd start on the way to being friends. It's absurd. I know this now.

And still I can't stop. I say, "Will you do it later?"

"I. Don't. Think. So," she says. Like that. And

then, into my face, "No. No, I won't. I won't do it later."

My face aches as if Pamela were squeezing it. That's it, I think. That's the end. I feel so bad.

But of course there's more to come.

In the mail, I have a letter telling me that the rent on the apartment is in arrears, and I'm endangering my tenancy. The letter says I should call the number above immediately. I read everything three times. *Arrears. Tenancy. Endangering.* I stare at those words. What if I didn't know what they meant? Then I stare at the signature. *Stanley J. Saxon, Senior Manager, Bradley Towers.* I read the letter three more times, and it still says the same thing.

Any moment, I might start screaming. I yank at my ears. They're burning, burning, burning up. I tried. I did. I tried so hard, and now everything is going wrong anyway. Three months in arrears! Burning ears! I probably have a terminal disease, I'm going to die, the first symptoms are burning ears. Arrears in my ears. Crazy words, crazy thoughts. Louise will nurse me through the illness, she'll kneel by my bed, holding my hand and kissing me on the cheek. Be brave, my little Em, I love you.

I crumple the letter and throw it across the room. I pretend it's not there. I walk away from it, try to ignore it, but I can't. I pick it up, smooth it out, read it one more time. Okay, I'll call him. I can do that. Just dial the phone and say, *Mr. Saxon, I'm looking for work. I'll pay as soon as I can.*

"I'm looking for work," I say out loud. "Looking as hard as I can, and I'll pay as soon as I can. I promise."

Is that enough to say? Will he let me stay then?

I don't know what I'll do if he puts me out. This is the first time the rent hasn't been paid. Even when she wouldn't let me out to work, when we had less and less money, even then the rent was paid on time, and I was the one who made sure it was.

I'll call and say I'm going to do the right thing. I'll say, *You can trust me.* I'll say, *Please, just don't put me out.*

40

Looking for work again. No. No. No.

It's raining, and the sidewalks glisten with tiny pink worms. At home I change my clothes and fill a plastic bag with the tiny segmented pink bodies. In the field, I dump them out in the garden, and they hurry to screw themselves into the earth. Gulls float overhead, like scraps of paper. They're hungry all the time. "Haaa! Haaa!" they scream.

"Hello!"

For a moment, I think it's the gulls again.

"Hello!" A woman pushing a shopping cart piled with blankets approaches me. "Hello!"

"Hello," I say slowly, standing up, thinking of Mr. Bielic. Did he send her? Foolish thought. Her feet are bare and covered with a thick crust of dirt. Her body is hidden by a black plastic garbage bag with arm-holes cut in it.

She stops in front of me. "Spare some change?" she says.

"No. I don't have anything."

She comes closer. An overpowering, unwashed smell drifts toward me. "I used to be like you," she says. "I looked nice like you. Better than you." Her voice is even, almost soft. "I wore nice dresses, not like that." She gestures at my torn jeans. "I wore earrings every day, a different pair every time. I had a beautiful house, better than yours."

"I believe you," I say. The thought comes that she is to me as I am to Louise: supplicant, beggar, someone desperately trying to convince someone else of her worth. I don't like this. I want her to go away.

"You sure you don't have any change? Where do you live? Can you go get me some money?"

"No," I say. "No money. None."

She walks away, pushing the cart roughly over the stony ground, then she stops and looks back, tapping her shopping cart, as if thinking of giving it to me. As if she knows that any moment now I'll be homeless like her.

I discover that worry is no color, not even gray. And no shape, although it feels long and thin, like a cylinder rolled so tight you can never unloosen it. I discover that worry sits on your shoulders like something metallic and inanimate, a dead weight, but also breathing and alive, waiting to sink its metal claws into you. It's a thing so real you should be able to grab it with your two hands, but you never can.

There are things you can do when you start worrying to stop yourself. You can:

Sleep a lot.
Look for work.
Watch TV.
Take a bath.
Go to bed early.
Look for work again.
Think about writing Louise a letter.
Write that letter.

> *Dear Louise,*
> *I only ask to be your friend, to see your*
> *smile.*

> *Your pure eyes tell me you haven't*
> *been hurt by life.*
> *I don't ever want to upset you.*
> *Love, Em.*

Think about Louise writing you back.
Write that letter, too.

> *Dear Em,*
> *It was so wonderful to get your letter.*
> *I hope to see you very soon.*
> *Much love to you from your new friend,*
> > *Louise.*

Tear up both letters.

Go to her floor, even though you have promised yourself you won't.

Walk slowly to her door. Make the experience last.

Hope you will meet her.

Hope you will not.

Think of things to say to her.

Tell yourself, Be real, she's not interested in you.

Memorize her door. It is not just a door. It is her door.

Say good-bye to her door.

Remind yourself no one knows what you're thinking.

Remind yourself you're not crazy.

41

"You gotta be ready," a man standing on a street corner bellows. He waves his arms in the air. "You gotta be ready, you folks, hear me." He's wearing a brown coat buttoned up to his neck, although it's a warm day. "You gotta be alert for what's coming down the pike, because they've fixed everything up in outer space. The government's got a secret program and you gotta be awake, alert, ready." He looks directly at me and starts again. "You gotta be ready, you hear me?"

Awake, alert, ready.

I am. At least, I'm trying to be. I remember Mr. Elias so long ago telling me to act upbeat and confident. I didn't have to really feel it, he said. I just had to pretend.

Awake, alert, ready, confident, upbeat.

Five good words. But none of them help.

"I'm looking for work."

"Sorry. Nothing."

I try again. Nothing.

Again. Nothing.

And again. Nothing.

I rest, sitting on the rim of a fountain outside a church. A group of teenagers prances down the street. The boys are big, thick, they look like hefty children suddenly grown tall. The girls have sunbaked hair, bright lips, they are like glowing animals. They touch each other, turn their faces to one another, like flowers, like deer, like dogs or cats. They talk and sing and leap into the air. They are probably my age. But they are young, so young. I don't feel old, exactly, but I don't feel young, either.

*   *   *

You try to think, but mostly you fret, and you don't know where fret stops and think begins, but this is what you think: You have no money, that's a fact, and you don't know what to do, although you've been trying to do the right thing, which is get a job, and you're scared, and you're tired from being scared and worrying and not eating enough. So you go to the market to buy food and you buy a lot of stuff — cereal, jam, cheese, bacon, eggs, bread — so much food, so much good food. And you want it, you want it all, you're eating it up already with your eyes, but you can't have it, even though you took it, even though you loaded up your basket, even though you brought it to the checkout counter. But when you open your purse, you see you don't have the money, and you say you'll just take the oatmeal and an orange, and the checkout girl with her stiff pink cheeks has to void the receipt and start over, and someone behind you says in a loud voice: You'd think people would check their purses before they went out of their houses, and your shoulders hunch in agreement, and you think that you could say you didn't want to check your purse, you didn't want to count your money, because you don't have anything left to count and you were just hoping there would be something in there, but you were wrong, and you go home with your orange and your oatmeal. And all of this makes you fret even more, and now you have more trouble than usual sleeping, and when you don't sleep you feel even worse, you feel so bad that there are almost no words to tell how bad you feel.

You feel all alone and wish someone would come and help you and save you, and you wonder where Father is and you even want Pamela back, and you think if you saw Sally in the street you would probably run up to her and beg for help. And if you knew where she and Father lived, you would go knock on their door. But even though you know where Louise D'Angelo lives, you don't knock on her door, because now you know she's not Louise the Angel, she wasn't sent here on earth to save you. Nobody was. Nobody will. That's just the way it is.

And then you think about the men coming to put you out in the snow, the way they did years ago when you had the apartment with Blossom Smith, although there is no snow now, it's spring, and the weather is warm, so even if they put you out in the street, you wouldn't freeze to death, and you could always go back to the shelter or the bus station, but the thought makes you cry and you lie on the couch and sob, and it's not even the kind of crying that makes you feel better in the end, and you say to yourself you will never go to those places or beg anyone, and then you think you'll be like that woman with the leather hands, with the filthy feet, with the terrible smell, with the plastic garbage-bag raincoat, telling people that you had a home once, also.

You think all these things, and you know it's all happening because you have no money. And you have no money because you have no job, and you have no job because Pamela made you stay home. But she's not here now and you still have no job, because you waited so long to look for one. Because you didn't want to think about it, and you pretended you didn't know that when she was gone you would not have a check every month, which was never very much, but which paid the rent and bought some food. And then you think that there's no check anymore because there's no Pamela. And no Pamela because you let her lie on the floor, you let her die. You didn't think about the check then. You thought . . . what did you think? You thought you would be free, that's what you thought, and if you thought anything else, it wasn't about checks or money. What did money matter, how much did you need, how much did you eat? Maybe you thought you were like a mouse that lives on scraps and crumbs.

42

I have my job-hunting rules. Out of the apartment by eight-thirty. Downtown by nine. Go around for three hours. Ask for work everywhere. Say you will do anything. You mean it, so you can say it. Don't stop. Keep going. After three hours, take a break. Eat something. Then go do it all over again.

Rules are good, they keep you going, but it's still the same old same old. I ask, they say no. *They* are the managers. They are all named Carl Richard Jeff, they wear tight jackets and tiny smiles and say, "Sorry nothing now try us again in a month keep in touch thanks for coming in."

At the end of the day, I stop in a dairy bar. "Double cone. French vanilla and chocolate almond," I say. I need something sweet, I really do. Something good, something nice, something that will make me feel better, because I feel lousy. I feel dispirited. I feel scared! What if I never get a job?

"You want two flavors on one cone?" the boy behind the counter asks. He's wearing a dirty white apron.

"Yes. Please."

"We don't give two flavors."

"What? I just want one scoop of French vanilla and one of chocolate al —"

"You can only have one flavor." He stares at me without expression.

"Why?" I want two flavors, French vanilla and chocolate almond. I really want both of them.

"You can just have one," he says again. "Which one is it going to be?" He taps the counter. His fingernails are long and dirty.

"Chocolate almond. Wait, no!" I feel anxious. I haven't given myself a treat in a long time. I shouldn't be doing this. I have to make the right choice. "French vanilla."

He bends over the freezer, straightens up, drops the mound of ice cream into the cone, and presses it down with a dirty thumb. "That'll be two-fifty." He holds out the cone toward me.

I stare at the ice cream. The mark of his thumb is right there.

"Two-fifty," he repeats.

"I — you — no thank you," I stutter.

"What?"

"I — I changed my mind."

"Hey!" he shouts. "Who are you? I fixed this ice cream for you. Take it!" His face is mean, and suddenly it's not a boy's face, it's Pamela's face, Pamela's lips drawn up in a feral snarl.

My own face is on fire. "You — you — you put your thumb in it," I get out.

My heart is beating like crazy. Am I wrong not to take the cone? Am I bad? Will I be punished? Maybe a drunk driver will cross the meridian and smash into me. A thunderstorm will take down high-tension wires and I will step on one. A stray bullet will find me as I take out my house keys. It will happen. I will be a body beneath a blanket, lying on the sidewalk, unattended, one bare foot sticking out. And all because I don't want to eat ice cream with his dirty thumbprint.

"Are you nuts or something?" He looks like he's going to leap over the counter and attack me.

Norma Fox Mazer

"Yes . . . nuts. Totally nuts." I back away and walk
out. Behind me, the boy yells something. I cross the
street fast and walk toward home. It takes me most of
the way before I start laughing. I think of his face, his
eyes bugging out crazily, and suddenly I'm happy, and
I feel good. I know I did right. Nobody should have to
eat ice cream with dirty thumbprints. That's another
rule of life.

Another day. My feet are sore, my eyes and legs ache.
I have been walking for hours, stopping in every store
and shop I pass. I hardly even hear them say "no" anymore. I walk in, I ask for work, I watch their eyes, I see
the refusal, and I walk out.

I lean against a garbage can, then sit down on
the curb. My arms hang, my head slides onto my lap.
Cars pass. *Swooooossss . . . Swooooossss . . . Swooooossss . . .*
I could be at the ocean listening to the water. Only I'm
not, I'm in the city, sitting on a dirty sidewalk, aware
of how much effort it takes not to let my mind slide
away into the white place, the numb place. It would be
so easy, like going down a chute-the-chute, arms out,
flat on your back, and no resistance. You just sliiiiide.
Down, down, down, and then for a while you don't
have to feel anything. I know all about it. How to let
myself down there. How to be stupid. How to float

above, watching as if it's someone else down there. How to feel nothing but a touch of pity for that girl there, that dumb one. But not be there, not there, not anywhere.

Don't, I say to myself. Not now. Don't do it. I make myself sit up. I clench my teeth and hold on. It's like getting a grip on a rope that's being yanked through your fingers, burning your hand. I hold on. I do it.

And then, I don't. I let go. And I slide, tired, too tired to stop myself. Tired of everything, of the same thing all the time, hope and disappointment, like the head and tail of a donkey, always yanking me in two different directions. Tired of getting nowhere, of always being stuck in the same place.

I drop my head to my knees and stare blankly at the gutter. Something small and silvery glitters up at me, and after a while I reach for it. It's a tiny tarnished pin in the shape of an oak leaf. I breathe on it, polish it against my sleeve. The donkey pulls me again, pulls me forward a little.

At home, I go through all the pockets of all the jackets and pants and skirts. I lift the pillows on the couch and crawl under the beds. I search the drawers, comb through the dark corners of closets and cupboards.

My take is two dollars and fifty-six cents. In the market, I buy baked beans, day-old bread, and spaghetti.

A man wearing gray sweats comes toward me, limping, waving, giving me a smile. In a moment I recognize him. St. Toothbrush. It's early in the morning, the air is bluish and cool still, the little leaves on the trees look black. I'm a little surprised to see him, but not that much. I touch my sleeve, where I've pinned the tiny oak leaf. I knew something good was going to happen, I just didn't know what.

"What happened to your leg?" I say. Not even hello. Just that, as if we know each other.

"I fell on some stairs." He answers the same way. "Wrenched my ankle. Not serious. Hey, it's great to see you. We never got introduced, did we?" He puts his hand out.

His name is Warren Weir. He wants to know how long ago it was it that we met. "I'm thinking it's about two months," he says. He's still got my hand. His hand is warm and soft, like a paw on a stuffed animal.

I tell him March. I give him the exact date and say I know it for sure, because it was the day before my sister's funeral. He looks sort of amazed and asks how old she was and if she was sick.

Twenty-two, I tell him. I know if he asks how old I am, I'm not going to lie. "It was a stroke," I say.

He whistles. His fat throat pulses. "Well, poor thing!"

Does he mean me or Pamela? *Me. Feel sorry for me, not her!*

Did he hear me think it? He's smiling at me in a certain way, and even though I smile back, I see that he's old, maybe as old as Father. His eyes are young, though. They're brown and they look directly at me.

Walking home, I think about him. I think about kissing him. And his eyes.

Sometimes Mother cried. Tears would appear suddenly on her face. I hated this. It frightened me. I'd pet her neck, bring her a cookie, a flower, beg her to talk to me, ask her why she was crying. "No reason," she'd say, sitting at the table, a cup of tea cooling in front of her. "Pay no attention to me, Em. It's okay. No reason, no reason." And the tears would go down her face.

She must have been sick of reasons by then. Reasons are like weeds, they grow and grow. There's a never-diminishing supply of them. But your heart gets tired of reasons, doesn't it, tired of waiting, of being patient and good. It becomes weary with its disappointments. It wants what it wants.

When I unlock the door, the apartment is dark and empty.

The apartment is empty. No one is in it.

Of course not.

But the emptiness comes as a surprise. As if I hadn't known. As if the emptiness is new.

The apartment is empty and this news comes to me, now, in this moment, as a shock — huge, final.

The apartment is empty. I know this. It is nothing new. It is empty of Pamela. It has been empty of her for months.

It is empty.

It will always be empty of Pamela.

Always.

She is quiet now. She is gone. She has left. Standing in the doorway, I understand this at last.

And then I understand something else: I am empty too. Like the apartment, I am empty of her. I understand, at last, that I am free.

43

A hand-printed sign in the window of the store says HELP WANTED. Inside, a red-haired man is crouched in front of a huge console TV, fiddling with the dials. "Hello," I say, "excuse me, I'm —"

He waves his hand at me. "Be with you in a sec." He turns up the volume and goes behind the TV. "Do you want something?" he asks in a moment, sticking his head around the side of it.

"I saw your sign."

"What? Can't hear you." He puts one hand behind his left ear. His cheeks are covered with large pockmarks, like the surface of the moon.

"Your sign," I repeat, louder.

"What about it?"

"I saw it."

"Uh-huh."

"It says 'help wanted.'"

"Right, I want help. You want to help me? Wait a second, it's only a joke. Help wanted, I want help. Get it?" He eases back on his heels. "You type?"

"Yes."

"Shorthand?"

"Yes," I lie.

He looks me over. "I put the sign up this morning. You're the first person that's asked about it. Some people say it's bad luck, taking the first person."

"Oh." I turn to go.

"Wait a second! Don't be in such a hurry. You think you'll be good for this job?"

"I'll work hard." I'm hungry, and my legs are starting to shake. This morning I found half an onion in the back of a drawer. I peeled off the soft, smelly bits and boiled it with dill seeds and drank it.

"Sit down," he says, pointing to a stool. "Don't be nervous. I'm not such a bad guy. What's your name?"

"Em. Em Thurkill."

"Tell me something about yourself, Em. Are you a good worker?"

"Yes."

"Why do you want this job?"

"Because ... because ... I want a job. I need a job."

"You have somebody to support?"

"Me."

"Well, I'll tell you what." He looks me over again. I have the sense that he takes in everything about me in that one moment. "I'm an old-fashioned guy — I do business on instinct and a handshake. You want to start tomorrow? Eight o'clock sharp."

"I have the job? When do I get paid?" I blurt.

"The usual is the end of the week. But what do you say I give you a little something as advance against your first week's pay?" He hands me a bill. Then another.

I stare at the money. I should stuff it in my pocketbook and leave before he changes his mind. "I can't take this."

"Sure you can. I told you, I have an instinct. You're not going to run out on me."

"I lied to you. I don't know shorthand."

"You don't?" He looks disappointed, then shrugs. "Don't worry about it. You can make up your own shorthand. I only do two or three letters a week, no big deal. What do you say, you want this job or not?"

I nod. I can't speak. Of course I want it. Doesn't everyone want it? Isn't he an angel, the true angel I've been looking for? Why aren't there hordes of people here, pushing me out of the way, jostling me aside?

44

"See this here, Lana? This is a weed. You want to take out a weed? Okay, here's the way." I close my hand over hers and we pull the weed together. "Carefully! Don't pull anything else. We're just going to take out the weed. There!" I hold it up. "We did it."

"Good for us," she says.

"Right. Now get your hands out of there."

"I want to pull another weed," she says.

"Okay, we'll do it together."

We do, and then I let her pull her own. She holds

it up like I did and looks it over. Then she says, "What's a weed?"

"You don't know what a weed is?"

She shakes her head.

"A weed is a plant, but it's the kind that takes up room from the plants we want to grow."

"Like flowers?"

"Right. Flowers and veggies."

"Veggies!" She glances at me, then caresses the tiny glossy spinach leaves that have poked through the ground. "What else does that weed do?"

"Well . . . it gets its roots in the soil and sucks up all the good soil food."

"Beat its butt," she said. "Beat its nasty butt."

On the street, I see a baby in a stroller, wheeled by its mother. The baby's legs toss about and its feet tap rhythm against the drum of air. Naked, solid, clean, brown, fat little feet. I want to run and kiss them. Wasn't I like that once? Didn't I also have baby feet once? Didn't Pamela? Didn't Mother and Father and even Sally? I'm disturbed and thrilled by this thought which seems, all at once, to contain the whole secret and puzzle of life. Baby feet.

45

I dream of Pamela on the ceiling. She sneers at me, heavy arms crossed over her chest, furious about something, but I don't get what it is. I notice slabs of ice all over the place, mini glaciers glittering like cold jewels.

Beautiful, I cry, and wake up.

My eyes go straight to the ceiling. A shaft of light pierces it diagonally. Otherwise, it's empty.

The clock ticks. I stretch and listen to the silence inside, the Saturday morning sounds outside. Yesterday was my eleventh day with Mr. Becker. I have food in the refrigerator and a money order made out to Stanley J. Saxon, Senior Manager, in the mail. It's not all the rent money I owe, but it's a beginning. Next week, I'll send another money order. I get up, thinking about the day, thinking *Once more. Let me try once more with Louise.*

"Hello," I say, and stand up. "Hello, Louise." I've been sitting on the landing for an hour, waiting for her to come down the stairs.

She walks by me without a word.

I go down the stairs behind her and into the lobby. "I would like to talk to you," I say to her back. She goes outside. I do too. "I don't want to be a pest," I say.

She looks at me. "But you are." Her eyes are like little blue plates with fine lines etched all around the perimeters.

"I'm working," I say. "I found a job. A wonderful job. I was looking for a long time."

"What are you doing?" she says. "Are you following me again?"

"No. I just want to talk to you. Can I talk to you?"

"Why?"

"I like you," I stammer.

"You don't know me. And if you did, you'd know I'm not that likeable. I'm not that nice a person." Her face seems to tighten and shrink; her cheekbones look polished. It reminds me of something, but I can't remember what. "I don't know what you've got in your mind about me," she says. "Maybe you're looking for a mother. Is that it? Where's your mother? What's the matter with her?"

"She's . . . gone."

"That's too bad, but let me tell you something. Don't look to me to be your mother substitute." Her voice is tight, sharp, clear. "I haven't done that well in the mother department. I have two daughters, and they both live as far from me as they can get. They don't like me, and you won't, either."

"I will," I say. "I do."

"No, you're wrong. You're foolish and wrong! Can I put it to you any plainer than that? One of my daughters I haven't heard from in a year. Okay? The other one calls me every two or three months. She tells me the news she thinks fit for my ears and hangs up. She never asks me anything. Not interested. So forget me. Because I'm not interested, either."

I look at her. "I still like you," I say. And I walk away.

46

Mr. Becker buys and sells used TVs, microwaves, CD players, stoves, and refrigerators. Every inch of the two floors of his tiny straight-up building are jammed with appliances and boxes and signs. BEST BUY IN THE WORLD. BECKER CAN BE TRUSTED. My office is a desk in a corner of the room near a window looking out on the street.

Just as he said the first day, two or three times a week he dictates a letter, which I take in "shorthand," and then type on the word processor. I use my own code. "Ubplno" stands for "You will be pleased to know." I make up new ones all the time.

I answer the phone, of course. "Becker's Best Buys! Good morning! This is Em." I take messages and give out information about models and prices from the big book he keeps on his desk.

I sweep and dust and sometimes I do little errands for him on my lunch hour, buy things for his kids or pick up the morning newspaper. I know I'm supposed to mind doing that, but I don't. I don't mind doing anything for Mr. Becker.

I also cut out the Becker ads he runs in the Friday and Sunday papers and paste them into a scrapbook. Sometimes I wait on customers, and I tell them they can count on Mr. Becker's word. Every morning around ten o'clock I go across the street and buy a container of coffee and two cinnamon doughnuts for Mr. Becker. And at the end of the week, he thanks me for being such a terrific worker and gives me my pay. I don't want this job to ever end.

47

On the way home from work, I stop to watch a soft-ball game in a school field. The girl at bat has dark hair pulled back in a stiff ponytail. She stamps her feet, bites her lip with small sharp teeth. The sky is that common radiant blue of early spring. The pitcher loops the ball toward the batter and she hits it hard into the outfield. Everyone yells as she runs toward first base. "Go, go, go!" they yell. She slides into second base on her belly. "Saaafe," the umpire, a tall man, bellows, stretching out his arms.

I stand by the wire fence for a long time, watching the game, watching especially the dark-haired girl. Me, I think, me in another life.

On the way home from work, I look into the window of a diner, an old railroad car, and see St. Toothbrush sitting at the counter. I'm sure it's him, although all I can see is his broad bent back. I go to the corner, and then I turn around and go back.

In the diner I sit down on a stool next to him.

He's got a cup of coffee and a newspaper, and he's making little concentrated grunts at whatever it is he's reading.

"What can I get you, honey?" the counterman says.

"Coffee."

"Anything else?"

"No, thanks."

Warren looks up. His round, brown, baby eyes are set deep in the soft flesh of his face. "Hey, this is nice, meeting you again. Where'd you come from?"

"I'm on my way home from work."

The counterman brings my coffee. "Anything else?"

"No, thanks."

"They have great pie here," Warren says. "The apple pie is the best."

"Homemade," the counterman says.

"Do you have elderberry?" I ask.

"It's too early. Not in season yet. We have apple, peach, cherry, banana cream."

"Apple," I say.

"And one for me too," Warren says.

We sit there and eat pie and talk.

Afterward he walks home with me and says goodbye and then comes back and asks for my phone number. "Is it all right if I call you?" he asks. "I mean, is it all right?"

On the way home from work, I stop in the market and buy fresh fish. At home, I make myself a perfect supper. Fish, salad, bread. Vanilla ice cream for dessert. I set the table, but then I don't sit down. I take my plate and stand by the window with it. And watch the phone, waiting for it to ring.

48

All day the windows of my office stream with rain. When I say good-bye to Mr. Becker, rain is still falling in long gray sheets, and the streets are slick and shiny. I walk fast, huddling into my sweater and looking over my shoulder for the bus. I don't have an umbrella. I need a lot of things I'm putting off buying until I've caught up with the rent payments. My feet are soaked in a moment, and halfway home the sole of my left shoe comes loose, flapping with every step I take. At a corner, a car passes too close, sending a flaring skirt of water over my legs. It's too much, and I duck into a store for shelter.

It's dry and warm. A heater hums somewhere. There's a peculiar smell in the air, something between old cellars and mustard. I've stepped into a thrift shop crowded with racks of clothes and bins of hats and sheets and toys. I walk down an aisle and stop in front of a shelf full of shoes. Red, black, green, purple, even silver. A pair of humbly ordinary white sneakers catches my eye.

"Try them on, darling!" A blonde woman sitting on a couch in the middle of an aisle winks at me. She's wrapped in something loose and gold colored. It looks like a pair of old drapes. "Go ahead!" she urges.

I don't really want to buy someone else's discarded shoes. She moves over to make room on the couch for me, takes the sneakers and inspects them. "These look good," she says. "Almost new, darling! Come on now, give them a try. You need something," she adds, looking at my feet.

The sneakers fit as if they were made for me.

"I knew it," she says triumphantly. "I've got an eye."

I laugh. "I guess you do."

We sit there talking, both of us hoping the rain will stop. When I finally leave with the sneakers in a plastic bag, the rain is coming down as hard as ever. I've barely gone two steps when I recognize the woman striding in front of me holding up a big green umbrella. Louise. I don't know what to do — stay behind, go ahead, speak, or just pretend she's not there. I remember exactly her words the last time we spoke. *Not interested.* And how I couldn't let it be, how I had to keep trying. Almost begging. *I still like you.*

I lag behind, but at the corner the light is red, and we both stop. The wind comes up and blows the umbrella sharply at me. "Oh, sorry!" Louise says, turning, and then she sees who she's talking to. Her blue eyes narrow in weary exasperation, as if I've planned this, and in them I see displeasure, irritation, how very little she thinks of me. She pulls the umbrella closer to her shoulder, an ordinary gesture, but in it is Louise's dismissal of me. That's when I understand fully that I'm nothing to her but an annoying, clinging, beseeching burr.

I grab the plastic bag closer to my chest and nearly leap away from her and what I see in her eyes. I have the small satisfaction of seeing a look of surprise cross her face, and then I'm past her, springing down the street, running, leaving her behind. My shoes squish through puddles, the loose sole flaps, my hair falls in my face, but nothing bothers me. I'm weightless, moving through air, traveling without even touching the pavement. Pride, like a tiny engine on each ankle, carries me forward. *No,* I think. *No. No.* I'm thinking *No* so hard I don't see the taxi rounding the corner, heading straight for me. The blast of his horn sends me leaping for the curb, and he passes in a huge spray of water. I'm safe, but soaked again.

Behind me, I hear a voice. "You jerk!" It's Louise, shouting at the retreating cab. "He would have rolled right over you," she says. She holds the green umbrella over me. "He drenched you."

I push a wet bunch of hair behind my ears. "I'm fine," I say, and I walk away.

"Oh, for God's sake," she calls, "don't be so stiff-necked." I hear her running behind me. "You'll come down with pneumonia," she says, catching up to me. "Look at you, you're like a drowned cat. Get under this!"

We walk along without speaking, the umbrella bobbing like a green roof over us. I don't know what charitable impulse grabbed Louise, but as soon as we get to our building, I'm leaving. I'm not forgetting my *No.* I've said yes and yes and yes and yes too often and too long. Thanks, Louise, and good-bye. That's what I'll say.

"Listen, uh —" Louise breaks the silence. "I was a little harsh with you the other day. I'm sorry."

"That's all right. I don't care anyway."

She glances at me. "You don't have to be polite. I know I was obnoxious. I can get that way. I apologize."

I don't say anything, and she doesn't, either. And that's the way it is until we get to the building. There, in the lobby, William is holding down his usual place on the bench. "Oh, there's Em," he greets us. "There's Em. There's Em and Louise," he sings out.

Hearing our names joined that way, I can't help glancing at Louise. "Hello, William," I say.

"Hello, Em! Hello, Louise! Are you happy today?"

"I'm wet today, William," Louise says.

William roars with laughter. "That's a good one, Louise. That's funny, Louise. 'I'm wet today, William.'" He hugs himself, rocking. "Em, that's funny, isn't it?"

"Sure is, William." I open the door to the stairs.

"We're two wet girls," Louise says, folding the umbrella. "Louise and Em are both wet, William." She's never used my name before.

She walks toward the door. I hold it open for her, and we go up the stairs together.

49

Pamela wakes up from her nap fighting mad, says her head hurts, hurts like bitter hell. She sits in her chair and watches TV, and the picture is wavering *damn TV just when you want it fix it how long you going to make me wait* and now she's really upset. A bitter sweat smell comes off her. Ever since I came back from Vermont she refuses to shower more than once a week. She says water takes away her strength.

I work at the TV, jiggling the box, moving the antenna this way and that. *Aren't you done yet come on hurry up I need something to take my mind off.* I'm doing it, Pamela, doing it as fast as I can.

She sits forward on her chair, tapping her fingers against the iron frying pan, the one in which I'll make her an omelette as soon as I get the TV working. *Bitch you're trying to make me feel crazy get it fixed or I don't know what I'll do I'm telling you my head* — she bites her lip, moans. Blood runs down her chin.

I'm doing it, Pamela, doing it, honestly, hold on. *Don't tell me to hold on don't say that to me not me damn damn.* She sobs and slams the pan against her leg.

Pamela, don't do tha —

She throws the pan at me. It hits me in the breast.

I cry out. Can't help it. And she slides off her chair, just slides right down it and sprawls on the floor on her back.

Pamela?

Her mouth is open, but she doesn't answer. Just lies there.

I crouch near her, holding my breast. There's a thump on the floor. Mr. Foster, mad about the noise. Automatically, I thump back.

I move away, watch Pamela, wait for her to get up and come after me. I push the iron pan out of her reach and plan my escape. The bathroom, I think: it still has a lock.

Her left eye is fixed on me. She's up to one of her tricks, all right. She's watching me.

What? I say. What do you want?

Her foot twitches, and I wait.

The clock in the kitchen ticking.

Her eye fixed on me. Her mouth opening and shutting.

The TV blurring in waves of color.

Truck horns outside like ships at sea, like the hoarse voices of giants, like prehistoric animals calling each other.

A breeze blowing the curtains.

Her eye.

The sun going down. The room growing cool. Heat clicking in the pipes.

She doesn't move. Saliva drips from the corner of her mouth and makes a puddle on the floor.

In the darkness, I dial 911.

How long did it take me to call? Hours. Coldhearted, murderous hours.

Although when I look at the clock, it is minutes that have passed. I see minutes, not hours.

Can I believe myself?

*   *   *

At first I thought it was a trick. Then I saw it wasn't. The drool from the corner of her mouth convinced me. Seven minutes or seventeen or seventy had passed. They had gone and they would never come back.

I stand on the spot. Stand where she fell. Where she fell. That day. Where she lay, looking up. Lay that day. Lay looking up, not speaking. Unable to speak. Unable to scream. To move. To beg. To curse.

Unable.

I stand there. Stand on the spot, as if on her. Stand there and don't move, and remember. Remember it all. And say, Pamela, I'm sorry.

I am.

Sorry, and not sorry. Sorry she's dead. Not sorry she's not here.

She toppled off her chair and slid to the floor. I have thought of it so many times. That is exactly what happened. Threw the pan. Toppled and slid. Fast, sudden. Just like that. Thump. Bump. And Mr. Foster, on the fourth floor, pounding with his broom on his ceiling. And me waiting for Pamela to jerk upright and scream *Shut up old fart piss off* —

But she never got up.

50

Every summer, there came a weekend when Mother and I walked a mile or so to the abandoned railroad tracks to pick elderberries. We filled our empty coffee tins with the tiny black berries that grew abundantly along the thin bending branches. Mother said it was something she remembered doing with her own mother.

At home we sorted through the berries, cleaning out leaves and stems. They stained my hands and tongue and teeth purple. They were full of tiny seeds. And — "Sour," I said, every year, as I tasted.

"Who asked you to eat them raw?" Mother said in reply every year. We were both happy in those moments. "You watch me now, Em. I'm going to fix them up."

She stirred cup after cup of sugar into the boiling pot of berries and scalded a dozen little jars and spread out the red rubber rings. When she was done, we had sweet jam for the rest of the year to spread on our toast each morning. And, oh, it was so good.

About the Author

NORMA FOX MAZER is the author of *After the Rain*, a Newbery Honor book. She is a National Book Award finalist, winner of the Edgar Allan Poe Award, and twice the recipient of the Lewis Carroll Shelf Award.

She lives with her husband, author Harry Mazer, in Manhattan and Jamesville, New York.